SPEED FREAK

REVIEW COPY NOT FOR RESALE
Title: Speed Freak
Author: Fleur Beale
Price: $19.99
Publication Date: 6/09/2013
For more information please contact Hannah de Valda
on 021 265 66 55 or hannah@devalda.com

SPEED FREAK

FLEUR BEALE

RANDOM HOUSE
NEW ZEALAND

The assistance of Creative New Zealand is gratefully
acknowledged by the author and publisher

A RANDOM HOUSE BOOK published by Random House New Zealand
18 Poland Road, Glenfield, Auckland, New Zealand

For more information about our titles go to www.randomhouse.co.nz

A catalogue record for this book is available from the National Library
of New Zealand

Random House New Zealand is part of the Random House Group
New York   London   Sydney   Auckland   Delhi   Johannesburg

First published 2013

Design: Megan van Staden
Cover photograph: iStock (file15467134)

Printed in New Zealand by Printlink

This publication is printed on paper pulp sourced from sustainably grown and
managed forests, using Elemental Chlorine Free (ECF) bleaching, and printed
with 100% vegetable-based inks.

CHAPTER ONE

IT WASN'T THE best of beginnings for me with my Year 11 science teacher. I stalled on the starting grid, sort of thing.

Mr Taylor was new to the school. We had our first science class with him a couple of days into the year. I came in late from lunchtime.

'Name?' he barked while taking a swift look at my bandaged arm.

Before I could reply, my mate — my good mate — Colin piped up from the back row. 'That's Archie Barrington, sir. Our very own boy racer.'

Thanks, Colin.

Well, that did it for Mr T.

'Sit there.' He pointed at a desk set by itself at the side of the room. 'That's the seat reserved for anti-social louts with no concern for the rest of us.'

Colin was grinning his face in half. I just shrugged and sat down. Mr Taylor looked slightly surprised. Maybe he expected me to argue. He kept glancing at me every few minutes during the lesson. A couple of times I caught a look of complete bafflement. I was being such a good little anti-social lout.

Colin was still spitting with laughter when we left. 'He's going to be mad as a wasp when he finds out.'

'You're such a pal. He'll hate me forever now. You too, you dumb ass.'

'Nah, it's all good. So how's the arm?'

'Fine. They took the stitches out this morning.'

'And you'll be racing again on Saturday.' He shook his head as if he didn't understand, though he was the guy who'd chopped the cast off his own wrist so he could keep on playing rugby.

The rest of the day passed without drama. Our English teacher knew me from last year, and all she said about my arm was, 'I trust it won't keep you from writing, Archie.'

'Writing's good, Ms Fielding. Mobilises the muscles.'

BACK AT HOME, Dad had left instructions for dinner that involved more muscle mobilisation. So far, so normal.

He came in around six, gave his hands a scrub, shoved my homework further down the table and served our dinner.

'Mmm, good!' He prodded the chicken. 'You cook almost as well as you drive.'

'It must be all the practice I get.'

He started getting very interested in the food on his plate. 'Yes. Well. We need to talk about that.'

'Nothing to talk about. It's sweet.' He put so much time into me and my kart, not to mention the money, I figured it was only fair I did my share of cooking. But my radar was bleeping off the scale. I hoped he wasn't going to say what it looked like he was psyching himself up to say.

He got over the plate-gazing stage and said it. 'I'm going to ask Erica to move in with me. With us.'

Shit. But I'd guessed this would happen sooner or later. I'd just hoped it would be after I was off at uni. 'Erica *and* Felix?'

'Of course *and* Felix. She's not going to dump a seven-year-old out with the rubbish.'

'So when does this happen?'

'Nothing's settled. We've talked about it. That's all. I told her I'd have to square it with you first.'

I thought about it while I finished my food, then I said, 'Mum left because of karting.' Among other things, but the time Dad put into karting was a big part of it. 'I haven't noticed Erica out there in the weekends. Isn't this a hope-over-experience situation?'

'She says she doesn't mind. We're not joined at the hip and she's got her own interests. She works some weekends anyway.'

Erica was a doctor, and if Dad had asked me, which he hadn't, she was about as bad a choice for him as Mum had been. 'She gets free babysitting as part of the deal?'

Dad waved that away. 'No. Her current arrangement stands.'

I picked up our plates and headed for the sink. 'You know what'll happen? You'll start giving up weekends here and there. Or you won't, and she'll leave.'

'You're all right with her moving in, then?'

I leaned against the sink and eyed him. 'No. But it's your life. I've got nothing against her. She's okay. Felix is so quiet you can hardly see him.'

Dad said, 'Tell it like it is, son. You're worried you won't be able to keep on with the karting, aren't you?'

I just nodded. I had such dreams. Formula 1, of

course. So many drivers had come up through karting. But more than that, I just liked the speed. And then there was that urge to win, to be the best, to do something really well.

Dad came over, gave me a one-armed shoulder hug and said, 'I've spelled it out to Erica. She knows the score. Well, what do you think?'

I took a few deep breaths. 'Just don't go having sex where I can hear you. And keep the public displays of affection on low revs.'

And so ended the day. I was facing a de facto step-mother and step-brother, and tomorrow I'd be back in the desk saved for anti-social louts.

CHAPTER TWO

IN THE MORNING I took the bandage off my arm. Yep, it'd be strong enough to race tomorrow week, when we were going up to the Manawatu track, just out of Palmerston North, for their club day. I was desperate to go. The club was hosting the first round of six in the Junior Challenge series the following weekend.

I wanted to get in all the practice I could, because winning the Challenge would be my chance to race at least once in Europe. It would still be expensive, but the winner got their airfares paid and they got supplied with the kart, the tyres — everything. That was my goal for the year — winning the Challenge.

I'd spent the holidays chasing sponsors. I'd put all my efforts into it, seeing as how Dad wouldn't let me get in the kart. 'Not till that arm's completely healed,' he said every time I suggested going out to the track. It was such a stupid injury — a bunch of us were at the beach, went scrambling around the rocks, I tripped on my jandal and fell. It wasn't far — just far enough to crack a bone and rip shit out of the skin. But if I nailed the sponsorship as a result, it could be worth it, because this year was going to cost a bomb, going to all six rounds spread throughout the North Island. On Friday — tomorrow — I had to front up to the firm that was my best hope of getting something more than just ten bucks and a pat on the back. My nerves twitched. I so didn't need the Erica drama distracting me.

A nasty idea hit my brain. How soon would she want to move in? Dad would help her. Of course. It would have to happen on a weekend, and the weekend that started the day after tomorrow was the only one we had free for the next few weeks. Somehow I couldn't see him waiting that long.

Bugger it all. I *knew* this was a bad idea. I parked it at the back of my mind and got myself to school.

The first bell went, and so did my phone. It was a text from Dad: *Howz arm? Practice tonight?*

Dumb question but I texted back before he could change his mind. *Arm fine. C u afta schl.* Brilliant — something for an anti-social lout to think about.

We had science straight after interval. Colin and his girlfriend Ginnie headed for the back row, while I went to the lout desk. Mr T didn't comment. He put the rolled-up chart he was carrying down on the bench in front of him and blasted off with the lesson.

'Today will be a brief departure from yesterday's topic. We're going to examine the workings of the internal combustion engine.'

Interesting. Very interesting.

He unrolled the chart and stuck it to the whiteboard. I started to laugh. The rest of the class guffawed and I could hear Colin shouting, 'Good one, sir!'

It was a diagram of a kart engine, with a panel of photos of the make of kart I drove down the side.

Mr T didn't crack even a glimmer of a smile. He just got on with explaining the parts of the engine and how it all worked. Then he finished up by saying, 'It takes a great deal of skill to drive these things. Sometimes people get things wrong and get injured. I guess it's like other people jumping to the wrong conclusion based on insufficient evidence.' Then without even a pause, he went on, 'Archie, you can move seats, although I'd advise you not to sit next to Colin MacPherson.'

I gave him a grin and went and sat next to Colin.

At the end of the lesson I walked past Mr T and said, 'Smooth, sir. Very smooth.'

'I'm pleased you approve, Archie.'

When we got outside, Ginnie said, 'I would've told him yesterday, but Colin shut me up. And you! You just sit there and take it!'

'I knew he'd find out sooner or later.' But it was pretty much how I lived my life now — using the things Dad had bashed into my mind about karting since I was six years old, the main one being *Keep your cool and wait till the other bugger makes a mistake.*

At lunchtime, Colin asked, 'What's up?'

I shrugged. 'Nothing.'

'Liar,' said Ginnie. 'You've only opened your gob to stuff food in it.'

They waited for an answer, along with the other three in our group — Nina, James and Silas.

'Dad's asked the girlfriend to move in.'

'Any kids?' Nina asked.

'Felix. Aged seven.'

'Could be worse,' Silas said.

'Easy for you to talk. You don't have to—'

Colin jumped to his feet. 'Come on. Let's chuck a ball around. Good for your arm, Archie.'

So I exercised my arm and put thoughts of Erica to the back of my mind.

DAD WAS WAITING when I got home. We lifted the kart into the trailer — it was an old garden trailer that he had converted. Craig, who was my top rival, had one that probably cost more than Dad earned in a year. But I was fine with our trailer — it had character.

I spent a few moments thinking about Craig. If I could beat him this year, there was a good chance I'd win the Challenge. The guy had his faults, but he was a top driver. Unfortunately.

'I hope nobody else is on the track,' I said.

'Won't worry us. We'll work with whoever's there.'

But I loved having it to myself and just driving. There was nothing like it: me, the kart, the speed and the track.

'What's your plan for this year, Archie?' Dad asked. 'Your driving style, I guess I mean.'

'Go like shit and don't crash,' I said.

He laughed all the way through Upper Hutt. We were almost at the track when he said, 'I won't buy new tyres yet. Not till we see how it goes with the sponsors tomorrow.'

I felt that kick of nerves in my gut again. 'I'll do my best, Dad.'

'I know you will.' He held up a hand. 'And no — I don't want to hear your speech just one more time.'

Fair enough. He probably knew it by heart now too.

We drove up the hills to the turnoff. The side road narrowed and the surface wasn't one I'd want to race on. We came round the final bend to see a four-wheel drive with a trailer parked sloppily by the clubhouse. The owner was driving his kart round the track.

'Damian Church,' Dad said. 'Let's hope he does the

decent thing and lets you have a go.'

'I could get on the track too. Plenty of room for both of us.'

'You know the rules, Archie.'

Yeah. I did. They said you couldn't mix senior drivers in with juniors. That rule was designed specifically to stop innocent drivers like me from tangling with people like Dangerous Damian. The guy had no feel for the kart, the track or the race.

We lifted my kart out of the trailer. 'Engine seemed okay when I tested it at home,' Dad said. We knew that didn't always mean it would be perfect out on the track.

I pushed the kart on to the dummy grid, then both of us stood at the side of the track in a spot where Damian couldn't avoid seeing us.

It took him a good ten minutes before he decided to come in. Dad shook his head a few times, and as the kart cruised into the pits he said, 'He drives like a drunk turkey. Off you go, Archie, before he can suggest a race.'

I slid into my seat and exited the grid as Damian rolled to a stop.

I took it easy for the first couple of laps, just warming up the tyres and getting the feel of the kart again after the long break.

Lap three, I got moving. Each corner, I hit my braking points spot on, nailing the apexes and exiting smoothly. The blur of the world outside, the roar of the engine, hands on the wheel — my idea of heaven.

Lap six, Damian waved at me to come into the pits. I guessed what he wanted — *a nice little race, Archie. Just the two of us.* I ignored him.

Next lap, he pulled out of the dummy grid in time to get up speed before I caught him. The prick! He'd had his turn — he should stay off until I'd had a decent run. He'd be sorry, I'd make sure of that.

I chased him down the straight. He made it round the right-hander at the end, but I gained on him with smooth driving whereas he kicked the tail out and turned in too sharp. I followed him down the back straight. He'd be easy pickings at the sweeper, but he wasn't messing about now. I checked the speed on the data logger: 107kph.

We arrived at the sweeper. Damian hit the brakes, turned the wheel too hard and spun.

I found myself following him. The world turned around me, once, twice, before I got control. I wasted more time by hitting the steering wheel and yelling, 'Stupid moron blockhead!' Me, not Damian. I should know better than to get caught up in a mangle like that. I did know better. Dad would be shaking his head — unless he was furious at me for not coming off.

I got my temper and my kart back in line. Focus. That's what I needed to do.

Damian was very experienced at taking off after a spin and I didn't catch him until we got to the S's. This time, I kept hold of my wits. I watched the gap, not the kart in front of me. I overtook while he was still wallowing around trying to find a line — any old line — through the corner. He wouldn't catch me now.

I turned my attention to driving consistent lap times. The consistent driver will often do better than one who goes hard out all the time.

After I'd done fifteen laps, Dad signalled to come in, and that's when I stopped playing it safe. I gave it everything, pushing the limits of the kart and my skill on every corner. There's nothing like it — the sheer joy of speed, of responding to the kart and the track, of driving without conscious thought.

I stayed on the track, too. Always useful.

I slowed and drove into the pits. Damian kept on circling the track, making the same blunders on each corner. He was probably hoping we'd disappear before he had to come in, because he knew bloody well that Dad would give him a bollocking. Dad might give me one as well, but not for racing Damian.

But he didn't say anything until we were about to drive away, when all he said was, 'Well?'

'Yeah. I know. I spun because I was looking at him instead of looking ahead.' I felt dumb, as if Damian had rubbed my face in the dirt.

'A useful reminder. Kart okay?'

'Sweet.'

'Stop kicking yourself, Archie. That turned out to be a timely lesson. Learn from it.'

'Yeah. I sure will.'

'Better today than on race day,' Dad said.

I shuddered. 'I reckon I owe old Damian a beer.'

'How's the arm?'

I cradled it and groaned. 'Really sore. Much too sore to cook dinner.'

'Never mind,' said my heartless father. 'Make yourself a sandwich. I'm going out with Erica.'

They'd be settling the moving-in business. I wouldn't let my mind go to what else they might do. The thought of him and Erica round the house — my home — getting all strokey and kissy almost put me off the idea of food. But not quite.

I started cooking the minute we got back. I reckoned the smell of frying onions and sausages would be torture to a hungry bloke who wasn't going to be eating for a half hour or so, but I made sure the sausages were too raw for him to steal one out of the pan.

I don't think he noticed. He bounced out, all showered and tidy, gave me a one-armed hug and disappeared to Erica's. Out of habit, I cooked a heap of veg. That was another thing Dad hammered into my head on a monotonous basis: *Watch your diet. Keep fit, keep lean, keep strong.*

CHAPTER THREE

I SPENT THE evening checking the website to see who I'd be racing against at Manawatu in the weekend. There were only going to be eight in my class, and I knew them all. I was reasonably sure I could beat them all too.

I jumped on to Skype and called a few of my karting buddies. Jack from Rotorua was as optimistic as ever. 'I'll be after you this year, Archie.'

'So what's new? You're always *after* me.' Of all my mates, Jack spent the most time off the track when he should have been on it. He'd spin out and have to sit in the paddock waiting for the truck to take him and his kart back to the pits. 'You'll be competing in the Challenge?' That was a surprise.

'Might be. All I've got to do is beat you this weekend and the old man'll be putty, mate.'

'I'm real worried, Jack. You can probably hear the old knees knocking.'

'Well, here's something to worry you. Craig reckons he's as good as stitched up a sponsorship deal.'

'The prick! He never said. And I talked to him on the weekend. Who with?'

'He wouldn't say, but judging by the hints he let drop, it sounds like a nationwide automotive parts outfit.'

Out of long habit, I kept my mouth shut. But bugger

it all, if Jack was right, then Craig and I were chasing the same sponsors.

Jack was never one for keeping his own mouth shut, and I knew he'd be after more gossip to spread around. Yep. 'Well? Aren't you worried? You know Craig — he'll probably get what he asks for.'

'Good luck to him.'

'Come on, Archie! You must be gutted. He talked like it was a done deal.'

'It probably is if that's what he's saying.' I grinned at him. I knew he wanted to reach into the computer and drag information out of me.

He tried another tactic. 'You should be worried, Archie. He's good.'

Yes. He was. For the past year it had been either him or me on the podium in first place. 'I won't make it easy for him.'

'So tell me something I don't know. See you in the weekend.' He logged off without a goodbye, a bit pissed off that I hadn't filled him in on my own sponsorship plans.

My meeting with the nationwide automotive parts firm was scheduled for after school tomorrow. My gut clenched. Had they already made up their minds to sponsor Craig?

I sat for a minute thinking about it. 'Come in for a chat,' they'd said. I knew what that meant: *Tell us why we should throw good money at you and not at somebody else.* I was well prepared. Poor old Dad had listened to my spiel about how wonderful I was at least ten times. I was tempted to go over it again — talk to the curtains, persuade them to sponsor me, seeing Dad wasn't around. But no — best not over-think it. I didn't want to come across like a goddamned parrot.

I distracted myself by skyping Selwyn. We only met at Nationals and Secondary School Champs because he lived in Dunedin, but we'd been friends since we were about eight years old when Dad took me to my first South Island meeting.

'Heard about Craig?' I asked.

'Falls on his feet, that one,' Sel said. 'If anybody doesn't need sponsorship, it'd be him.'

Damn. It seemed like the entire karting world was behind Craig, but all I said was, 'True. You know, he should be a real wanker. Stinking rich father. Everything given to him. Pity he's such a decent guy. Hard to hate him.'

We had a bit of a moan about how our own fathers had jobs that didn't bring the dollars rolling in. Dad owned an aluminium joinery outfit. Sel's father was a mechanic.

My last and longest Skype call of the evening was to Kyla. If we lived closer we'd probably have hooked up by now. She was cool, and funny and a babe. On the track, she showed no mercy and she was an ace driver. But she lived on a farm near Wyndham. The first time I'd met her I didn't admit I hadn't a clue where Wyndham was, but I looked it up when I got home. Way the hell south, not far from Invercargill.

I've raced in Invercargill. It's a long, long way from Wellington.

We were just about to say goodnight when she said, 'I knew there was something I meant to tell you. You remember that girl called Silver?'

'The chick from Christchurch? What about her?' She'd stopped karting a couple of years ago but it was hard to forget a name like Silver.

'She's back and she'll be racing against you. According to reliable gossip, she's going to do the Challenge.'

'Silver Adams. She was pretty good. She must be serious about it if she's conned her old man into doing the Challenge. It'll cost a bomb, all that travelling up to the North Island. What about you? Any chance of you doing the Challenge?'

She laughed at me. 'I don't have your dreams, Archie. All I want is to drive fast, drive well and win.'

'But I'd see you more often if you entered the Challenge.' Six times a year instead of one or two if we were lucky.

'There is that.' She sighed and looked wistful. 'But no. Dad can't take that much time out from the farm.'

'Yeah. Sorry. Should keep my gob shut.'

'Hey, it's fine. Anyway, I don't want to race in Europe.'

We talked for another five minutes. I blew her the usual kiss and then logged out, wishing the kiss could be for real.

CHAPTER FOUR

THE FOLLOWING MORNING, Dad was all hyped and trying not to show it.

'Erica's going to move in, then?' I asked.

'She is indeed. Next free weekend.'

'Tomorrow?' Hell. I needed time to get my head around this.

He reached across the table and ruffled my hair, rubbing in about half a Weetbix along the way. 'Back up the trailer, Archie. I'm not that heartless. We've got a free weekend in March. It'll happen then.'

It was a done deal. It was going to take some getting used to.

'She wants her kid to get into karting, does she?'

Dad almost leapt at me to slap his hand over my mouth. 'Absolutely not! In fact, that's her one condition about moving in. She says if we try and get Felix into a kart, she'll move out.'

I gave him a look. 'And you told her we wouldn't? Come on, Dad! That's just freaking dumb!'

'No, Archie, it's not. She's seen too much carnage, and somehow it's all got mixed up in her mind and now she sees all motor sport as dangerous.' He shook his head. 'I don't even try and talk to her about it now. She just gets so upset. It's when she has to patch up kids who've been in car accidents — gets to her every time, she says.'

I just shook my head. The relationship wouldn't last. No way. He was crazy to think it would. Just shows what love can do. My face might have shown some of what I was thinking because he said, 'It'll be fine, Archie. Come on, you've got other things to worry about right now. Text me when you finish with those chaps this afternoon. And don't expect anything. Just do your best.'

It sounded exactly like one of his karting lectures.

School dragged. I kept thinking of stuff I could include in my *sponsor-me* speech, then I'd think *No, don't put that in.*

The final bell went and I pushed my way out of the building. Nina grabbed my arm. 'Are you always this jumpy before a race? It's a wonder you win anything!'

I stopped and stared at her. 'You, my friend, are a genius!'

She looked puzzled. 'Not that I'm arguing — but why?'

'Focus. It's all about focus. Being calm. In control. Goal in sight.'

She gave me a shove. 'Whatever. Good luck anyway.'

THE MEETING WAS much more formal than I'd been expecting. Five guys, all in suits, sitting at a long table and staring at me. They didn't ask me to sit down.

Okay. You want me to work for this? Right. I'll bloody work my arse off. Thanks to Nina, I was in my pre-race space, alert and ready to show what I was made of — one hundred per cent fighting mongrel.

The guy I'd already met introduced me. I walked across the room and shook hands with each of them, him included. I made sure I called each one of them by name and I looked each one of them in the face. Then I stepped back a couple of paces from the table.

'Right then, Archie. We've got your CV here along with your race record.' Brendon Schurrick, managing director, tapped the papers in front of him. 'What we need now is to hear why we should support you, and not, say, Craig Bateman.'

Did that mean the deal with Craig wasn't sewn up and signed off? A surge of adrenalin punched me. This was a battle between him and me, off the track this time. I intended to win it.

I put my hands behind my back and held my head high. 'It's going to be a fight to the death between Craig and me this year. We both want to win the Challenge, but I fight harder than he does.' None of that was what I'd planned on saying. Oh well, go with the state of the track and watch for when conditions change.

'You fight harder? Explain what you mean.'

Shit. I didn't want to bad-mouth Craig. I took a moment to work out how to explain. 'He's a fighter and he'll work hard for his sponsors. They couldn't ask for anybody better to back. Except me. I know how to fight too, but I also know how to work. I've always had to work for what I get. I've earned money by mowing lawns since I was ten. I cook dinner every school night, and I share the housework with Dad, fifty-fifty. I help out, earn what I can and he pays the rest of the karting expenses. That's the rule in my house. There's another rule — if I slack around at school he'll pull the plug on the whole deal.' I gave them a grin. 'He says it's character building.'

The guy on the end, Martin, asked, 'What do you say to that?'

'I tell him I must have one hell of a character by now.'

They all smiled, then Brendon said, 'Your mother's not in the picture?'

I shook my head. 'No. They broke up when I was six. She lives up the coast on a lifestyle block. She's into self-sufficiency. Doesn't like me doing the karting but she doesn't go on about it.'

Brendon pushed the papers into a tidier pile. 'Thank you, Archie. Can you give us a minute or two? We'll call you back shortly.'

I found the waiting room and made myself sit down when my instinct was to prowl and howl out *Sponsor ME!*

They didn't keep me waiting long. I walked back in, and this time they asked me to take the seat across the table from the five of them. I sat, making sure I didn't perch nervously on the edge of the chair.

The few seconds it took for Brendon to break the silence weren't exactly stress-free. 'Archie, you've impressed us.' I could almost hear the *but* waiting to fall out of his mouth. Sure enough, he went on, 'But we're not convinced that we wouldn't do better getting behind Craig.' He held up a hand to stop the protest I wasn't going to make. 'Yes, we do know that your records are fairly even, but there's little doubt we're looking at a future champion in him.'

To hell with that for a reason. I put both hands flat on the table. This was a fight? Right, I'd fight. 'And we all know why he's got a better chance than I have to keep going in motor sport. It's because his father's got the money to back him, to pay for the travel, the accommodation and everything that goes with it. My father hasn't. But I wouldn't swap my family for his. I can set up a kart, and I know for a fact that Craig can't because I've helped him sort out more than one problem.

'I know how to work. I already know how to fight for everything I get. I fight when I'm out there on the track. We both do, and we both fight fair. But I know what it's like to build your life around what your dreams are. I know what it's like to juggle my time so that I get the chores done and keep up with the schoolwork. I'm one hundred per cent committed to winning the Challenge. I want to be New Zealand Junior Champion, too. I want my name on that cup. I want to be the driver going to Europe. I'll work my butt off for both of them. And I'll work my butt off for you.'

I sat back, wondering if I'd said too much. Too bad. It was all true.

They said nothing, until Brendon glanced at the others, then asked me to wait outside again.

I flopped down in the waiting-room chair. Shit, this was tiring. Given the choice between this and cleaning the shower and the bog, I'd take the cleaning duty every time.

They made me wait longer before they called me back in. I sat down, couldn't tell a thing from their five expressionless faces.

'You're a most persuasive young man, Archie,' Brendon said, after an age-long silence. 'So this is what we've decided.'

I tried not to look hopeful. I know that I did look hopeful.

'We'll sponsor you for a full set of slicks for each of the first three Challenge meetings.'

That would be a help. A set cost around $300. 'Thank you, sir.' I tried to sound grateful rather than disappointed.

He must've seen through it, because there was a definite gleam in his eye as he went on, 'If you beat Craig at two of those three meetings, then we'll sponsor you for the rest of the series. New slicks for each race.'

I sat back, a grin busting out all over my face. 'You won't be disappointed. Thank you. Thank you all very much.'

Smiles all round. Brendon came with me to the door and shook my hand. 'You might like to know that you ticked all the boxes, Archie. We're pleased to be supporting you.'

I thanked him again, wondering what boxes I'd ticked. I sent Dad a text: *3 sets slicks*.

He texted back: *Helpful.*

I told him the rest of the deal when he got home. He rubbed his hands. 'That should spice up the competition nicely. You did well, Archie. I'm proud of you.'

'I've still got to win two out of three.'

'One race at a time. No point in bending our chassis out of shape over it, whichever way it goes.'

That night I got a text from Craig: *Congrats u arse!*

CHAPTER FIVE

SATURDAY MORNING, DAD rewarded me for getting the sponsorship by hauling me out of bed. 'Up you get, Archie. We're painting the spare room today. Get it all nice for young Felix.'

What that turned out to mean was me clearing the room while he went and bought the paint. My father has as much taste as a wet-weather tyre. He chose vivid yellow for poor old Felix.

'No,' I said. 'We are not making that kid live in an egg yolk.'

'What's wrong with it? He'll love it.'

'I bet you a weekend off cooking he won't.' Dad was always a sucker for bets that had the chance of letting him off the cooking roster. 'I say we get Felix here and we ask him.'

So that's what we did. Dad painted a wide yellow stripe down one wall while I rang Erica.

'But Archie — I'm at work and he's at his carer's. Why do you need him?'

I ran the egg yolk past her.

'An emergency situation. I'll call the carer and your dad can pick him up.' I was about to hang up when she added, 'Thanks, Archie. Thanks for looking out for my boy.'

Oh, crap. She was already moulding me into a big brother and he hadn't even moved in. She possibly hadn't factored in that I was a big brother who was a major speed freak. I went off to deliver the message to Dad.

Fifteen minutes later, Dad strode into the room, followed by Felix, who looked miserable.

'Take a look at that, Felix,' Dad said. 'A real man colour, eh!'

I eyeballed my father. 'Play fair, Dad. Get out of here and let Felix make up his own mind.'

Dad laughed but he ambled out. I shut the door on him. 'Right, Felix. I think this colour stinks. Dad thinks it's better than spaghetti. You're the one who'll have to live with it. Do you love it or hate it?' I gave him a friendly big-brother grin.

He looked at the floor, muttered something and a tear splashed down. Shit and double shit. I put an arm around him and turned him away from the ghastly stripe of yellow. 'How about we look at some colours? You can say if you like them. Okay?'

He gave the tiniest nod. I guided him out of the room. Dad took one look and changed his approach. 'Ah, I see that Archie was right. Win some, lose some. Looks like I'm on kitchen duty tonight.'

He came with us to the computer and the two of us had to clown around for about five minutes before we could get a peep out of Felix. Eventually, he whispered that he liked blue, and could he have orange doors.

HE ENDED UP staying with us all day. Dad gave him a small paintbrush, and he sat on the floor painting the skirting boards orange. Later, when Erica came for dinner, Felix showed her the room while Dad served up the meal. 'It's wonderful. I love it,' she said, but what she was really looking at was her kid's proud smile.

'Shy little lad,' Dad said when they'd gone. 'It'll be good for him to be around men more.'

'Well, he looks like being your soulmate,' I said. 'You've both got lousy colour taste.'

I figured what he really meant was that karting could be the making of Felix — bring him out of his shell and all that. Well, Erica knew her own kid — maybe she knew he'd run a mile from the roar of an engine. Still, it was tempting to think that if we did try and get him into it, she'd move the two of them out. But no, I'd told the sponsorship guys I played fair. So I would.

Felix was quiet and little. As my mates said, it could have been worse.

THE NEXT WEEK was full on. Every teacher took it into their heads to dump assignments on us. I cooked, mowed a couple of lawns, did my chores and slogged my way through the homework. There was no time to skype, except for short chats to Kyla. Maybe the workload at home would decrease when Erica moved in. I went off into a dream where she did all the cooking, hired us a cleaner and refused to let us touch the garden. Nice.

Dad put in quite a few Erica hours during the week. I didn't say anything, but on Friday after school I dumped my gear, changed into work overalls and took myself into the garage to do some prep on my kart.

I took the motor off, being careful not to ding anything. I set it down and picked up the spare. We'd take both engines tomorrow, as always. I bolted it on, connected the wires and hoses, then fired it up.

Except that it wouldn't fire. I began to go over it, checking everything I could think of, running through what could be causing it. Still nothing. The spark plug was almost new, so I left that alone. It shouldn't be the fuel mix because I was always careful to get the ratio of petrol to oil right.

I was standing back, frowning at it, when Dad came in. 'Shit! Sorry, Dad. I lost track of the time.' I waved a hand at the kart. 'That's the spare. It won't start. I can't work out what the hell it is.' I tried the starter again.

Dad said, 'You get the tea. I chucked corned beef in the slow cooker this morning. I'll sort this out. Don't worry, son.'

I handed him the spanner I'd been using. 'It's just . . . I want to do well this weekend. Nail that track. I need all the advantage I can get over Craig. He won't come down to Manawatu, but you can bet your arse he'll put in the practice on all the other courses. It'll give me a psychological edge if I can beat him next weekend.'

Dad took hold of my shoulders. 'Listen, Archie. The sponsorship's important. I'm not denying it. Those extra tyres would be bloody useful. But I want you to forget about that. Just get out there and race your heart out. That's all I ask. We'll buy the goddamned slicks if we have to. Stop worrying.'

It was enough to make a bloke choke up but I

managed to mutter, 'Thanks, Dad,' as I took myself off to the kitchen.

I was never going to win a cooking competition, but I got the job done, all the time turning over in my head what could be wrong with the kart.

I gave Dad a yell, mashed the spuds — and heard the sweet sound of the engine.

He came in as I was dishing up. 'What was it?'

'Let me get in the door, Archie.'

Damn it, he was in one of those moods when he'd tell me in his own sweet time. Still, I wasn't too worried. The engine was going and it had sounded good.

But after he'd done nothing with his mouth except put food in it for five minutes, I gave in. 'Everything's sweet now?'

'Yep.'

'Dad!'

He laughed. 'It was electrical. The starter motor brush wire was broken.'

I let out a sigh of relief — it wasn't going to take big money to fix. 'I didn't even think of that. Good call.'

Craig wouldn't know how much anything cost. He wouldn't even be interested. Dad was right — the battle to win the extra sponsorship was going to add a kick to the year.

Bring it on.

CHAPTER SIX

WE DROVE UP to Palmerston North on Saturday night, and there was a nasty surprise waiting for me at the motel — Craig came strolling out of the unit next to ours.

'Thought you'd turn up sooner or later,' he said.

'Didn't see your name on the entry list,' I said.

'Last-minute decision.'

I looked around for his kart trailer. 'Are you planning on doing the course on your own two legs?'

'I'd still beat you. Gary'll be here in an hour or so.'

'Gary? Isn't Carl your mechanic?'

'Gary's new. He's the best. Dad made him an offer he couldn't refuse. He'll be taking it easy. It's a long drive from Auckland.'

I didn't bother asking why Craig hadn't jumped in the van and come down with Gary. His father would have handed him the plane tickets — *Here you are, son. We don't want you getting tired by a long road trip.*

'Your dad's going to be here?'

He shook his head. 'Gary's doing the honours.'

Dad locked the van, then said, 'We're cooking dinner. Got enough for three. How about you join us?'

Old Craig's face lit up like a tail light. 'Cool! Thanks,

Bill. I was just going to order pizza.'

Dad tutted and treated him to the *proper food* lecture. I winked at Craig, and he grinned back. He'd heard the same lecture a few times by now.

Over dinner of cold corned beef, coleslaw, mashed spuds and broccoli — possibly a more basic feast than Craig was used to — conversation inevitably got around to the Challenge.

'Have to warn you, Archie,' Craig said, 'I'm planning on winning.'

'Plans are good,' I said. 'But it's the performance that counts.'

Dad just smiled, leaned back in his chair and listened to us sparring.

Craig and I dealt to the dishes — he did seem to know how to dry a plate. We'd just finished when we heard Gary pull up outside. Craig hung up the tea towel, thanked us for the meal and left. Through the sliding door I watched him go up to Gary and high five him.

'I'm glad you don't do that,' I said to Dad.

'What's wrong with a high five?'

'Not that. I reckon it must be lonely for Craig. Gary might be the best money can buy, but it's not like having your old man with you.'

My old man didn't respond to that, except to look pleased and tell me to make him a cup of tea.

WE GOT TO the track at 7.30 in the morning. Craig and Gary were right behind us.

We set up our base and unloaded the kart. I pulled

on my race suit, picked up a rag and rubbed it over the bodywork.

Dad took the rag from my hand. 'Calm down. Go and check out the track.'

I was a couple of steps away when he said, 'Archie, drive your own race. Don't worry about any other bugger.'

He was right, as usual. I couldn't let Craig get into my head. I couldn't worry about him beating me.

We took the kart to the tech shed for scrutineering. Gary and Craig were already there. Gary and Dad shook hands and I could tell they were sizing each other up — *I bet I'm a better mechanic than you are.* I caught Craig's eye and we laughed.

Jim, an old guy with frizzy white hair, was in charge of scrutineering. He checked the brakes, the steering, the nuts and bolts for tightness, and the transponder. After he'd tugged at it, I checked it myself just in case he'd loosened it. I always did that — useless going all out to win if the transponder fell off during the race and couldn't record my brilliant performance. But all was well. The little yellow box was firmly attached to the back of my seat just as it was meant to be.

The last of the drivers in our class arrived just as I was done with scrutineering. Next on the programme was the drivers' briefing, and after that there was nothing to do but wait for my first race.

I went outside to look at the track. We'd be racing anti-clockwise. It was tight and technical, a real driver's track and probably my favourite. Craig came out too, and we wandered around, both of us intent on memorising the course. At one point, he said, 'I warned Josh Gibbons to watch out at the end of that front straight. Told him to watch out for the love-taps.' Love-taps meant somebody was behind you, bumping the back of your kart, letting you know they wanted to pass you.

'You're so kind. Bet he didn't fall for it, though.'

'Just planting a seed of doubt, Archie. You should be grateful. That could earn us a tenth of a second on each lap.'

I tried a touch of psychological trickery myself. 'Are you worried Josh'll beat you?'

But Craig laughed. 'Nice try, Archie.'

The loudspeaker called our practice.

As always, Dad was the one to push the trolley with my kart on it down to the dummy grid. We didn't talk much, just a few comments about the weather, my position on the grid. Nothing earth-shattering.

Then we were into the tuning run, all of us doing our own thing as we spread out along the track, working on smoothness and speed instead of worrying about getting past the guy in front. Lap times weren't so critical on a club day with a randomised, pre-determined grid, but next week it'd be a different story. Best lap time would get pole position.

My kart felt good, though I was glad to know there was a brand new set of tyres waiting and ready for the first of the Challenge series.

Back in the tech shed, I waited for my turn to weigh in. I'd grown over the holidays, but I still needed lead on the kart to bring me plus the kart up to the minimum for our class. Craig was taller and heavier-built than I was, and when we'd raced each other a couple of months ago he'd been not too far off the minimum weight. If he grew during the year, then the power to weight ratio could well end up in my favour. Even half a kilo over the base weight would handicap him. I should start buying him ice creams.

My turn on the scales. No problem, but I knew there wouldn't be. Dad was very particular about keeping to the rules. The minimum weight of driver plus kart was 145 kg for the Junior Max, the class I was racing in. I still had a few kgs to go before I'd reach that without the help of the weights.

We took the kart back to base. There was nothing I needed to do since it was running sweetly. I gave Craig a yell, we picked up Josh on the way and wandered down to the notice board to find our grid positions for the first race.

'Shit,' said Josh. 'Look at that, will ya! I'm at the back. Again.'

We grinned at him, and Craig patted his head. The grid was worked out on a random mix format, and Josh knew perfectly well he'd be up the front at some stage during the day because there were only nine karts in our class.

He kicked at the fence. 'I hate being at the back first up. It's not a lucky start to the day.'

'You don't need luck,' said Craig. 'You need skill.'

'The back of the grid's okay,' I said. 'Think of it as the chance to practise your passing.' I liked starting well back and hunting my way to the front — working out how to pass, how to sneak through.

Josh didn't look convinced. We watched him run off to talk to his father, who seemed to say something that cheered him up.

'Archie, when will you learn to stop helping the opposition?' Craig shook his head. 'That kid's going to get competitive soon enough. You don't need to hand out the advice.'

Josh was twelve and it was his first year driving in the Junior class. He was a bit of a nervy kid, but he'd settle down. Just give him time.

I stuck a concerned expression on my face. 'I was right then? You *are* worried Josh'll beat you.'

Craig laughed. 'Shit scared.'

We joined Lewis and Tama at trackside to watch the cadet class. There were a couple of six-year-olds at the back of the grid with the big X on the back of their karts to show they were learners and, as yet, unrated.

Each competitor under eighteen had to have a parent or guardian with them on race day. For these little kids, that person also got to start the engine for their driver. The starter gave the signal, and the kids were off, leaving the adults to duck and dance out of the way as the karts roared away.

'Whoa! Yay!' The cry went up from the onlookers as one of the adults stumbled and nearly face-planted on the concrete. But he caught his balance and stayed upright to a round of cheering.

The kids didn't notice a thing. They roared off the dummy grid, and round the track they went, in formation, waiting for the signal to start racing.

'They're away!' Lewis yelled. 'Watch 82. That's Marina. My sister. She'll go off at the end of the back straight next lap. Betcha.'

'She's a barger,' Tama said as 82 bumped her way into a gap, shoving the drivers on either side so she could get through.

'No manners at all,' said Lewis cheerfully. 'Here she comes. Watch this.'

Kart 82 hammered down the straight — and went barrelling off on to the grass.

'What the hell was that about?' Craig asked. 'She didn't even try to take the corner!'

Lewis was laughing too much to answer for a couple of seconds. 'She was dead set on breaking my cadet speed record. I should have explained that I'd stayed on the track when I set it.'

We watched Marina jump out of her kart and push it further into the grassed area. She pulled off her helmet, scanned the spectators for her brother, then raised both thumbs. Her face was one beaming grin. Lewis clapped his hands at her and gave her the thumbs-up.

'Will you tell her?' Craig asked.

'Nah. She's too stoked.'

We watched the rest of the race. Already, even though those kids were so young, you could tell who the natural drivers were. There were at least a couple in the pack with the killer instinct. I'd be willing to bet that Marina would be good once she settled down.

We watched a couple more races, then it was our turn to collect our karts and take them down to the grid. I was in position five. Craig was next to me on six. I pulled on my helmet and climbed into my kart. Number 24.

This was the moment I loved. The helmet shut out the world, and it was just me and my kart. I stilled my mind, pictured the track, driving it in my mind. Next, I visualised the start. Craig would try to cut across me to the inside the second the lights signalled the start. I pictured myself hitting the throttle, sticking to the inside so that there was no room for Craig to muscle in. We'd probably catch the leading bunch at the corner. *Look ahead. Look at the gap, not the karts.*

I was ready.

CHAPTER SEVEN

WE LEFT THE dummy grid on the starter's signal. Round the track in formation for the rolling lap, watching for the lights at the start/finish line. They went out — and we were racing.

I opened up the throttle. Craig appeared in my peripheral vision. I held my line, hugging the inside. He fell back.

I kept my eyes on the track ahead. The leading four off the grid were bunched up until the corner, which they took in single file, the back markers losing valuable tenths of seconds. I'd pick off the slowest on the next corner.

I caught him on the back straight, staying in his slipstream until we hit the braking zone, when I pulled out smoothly and drove into the gap. One down and a tightly bunched group of three in front.

Sometimes you get lucky. The front runner lost power on the sweeper and pulled off the track. Two left and Craig hunting me down. The two in front were new to the game. I overtook one on the straight before the hairpin, and the other as we came out of it.

For a whole half-lap I was tempted to just race. I wanted to beat Craig. I wanted to be the winner on the podium. I wanted to be the one making the dumb speech at prize-giving. But thanks to the hammering Dangerous Damian had handed out the other night, I came to my senses in time and kept to the game plan Dad and I always used in practice. Grandad had helped us work it out. I didn't want to have to tell him that I'd chucked it on the rubbish heap.

I settled in to testing the limits. Craig got past me in the hairpin on the fourth lap when I went for a nice little excursion over the grass caused by turning in too soon at the entry point. No worries. I had those braking points, apexes and exits fixed in my memory now — they were those from the previous lap.

By the final lap, Craig was a kart length in front. He'd be happy, and cocky.

I shut him out of my thoughts. Now for the fast lap: the lap where I put it all together, went for speed and smoothness.

Craig was doing the same. It was a two-kart race, him and me with the rest of the field way behind. I watched ahead of me, kept him in my awareness, but he wasn't my focus. Into the corners, looking into the apex, flicking eyes ahead to the exit point. Always watching ahead of where I was on the track. Smooth, fast, focused.

The chequered flag ahead. Craig's kart in front of me. I pulled out from his slipstream, racing side by side to the finish line.

I think he got over first. Hard to be certain.

We drove round again, slowing the speed, into the pits and across the scales.

Dad met me, his face carefully expressionless. 'Craig won by a tenth.'

'He did? Bummer.'

'Everything okay?'

'Kart's good.' I checked the data logger for my times. 'Fastest lap is 45.085. That's not too bad. Cornering is okay too.'

'Practise the rest of the day as well,' Dad said.

I didn't say anything for a moment. I wanted to show Craig I was a better driver. Damn it, I just wanted to win. But — stick to the game plan, keep the focus on the main prize.

'Yeah. Okay.'

We went back to our base. Craig poked his head in the tent. 'Want to watch the seniors?'

'Off you go,' Dad said. 'Nothing to do here.'

I had a bet with myself that it wouldn't be long before Craig pointed out that he'd won. He was never obvious about it, always came at it from an angle.

'How's your kart going?' he asked.

I had a private smile. 'No problems. Yours?'

'Top notch. Gary's good. Almost worth what Dad's paying him.'

Josh came over to join us. 'How's it going, Josh?' I asked.

He didn't look happy. 'Awful. The engine's all to hell and we don't know what's wrong.'

'Tough,' Craig said.

'Come with me,' I said to Josh. 'We'll see if Dad can sort it out.'

Craig caught my eye and shook his head. Well, bugger him. Josh wasn't going to worry us for a year or so, and the two of us had been helped out often enough. It wouldn't kill him to let Gary the Great give the kid a hand.

Josh and I hung about, listening to the men trying to work out what was wrong. They still hadn't got it sussed by the time our next race was called.

'Ring Grandad,' I said. 'It's just the sort of thing he loves.'

Dad pulled out his phone as we headed to our tent. 'Come with us, Josh. If he's got an idea, you can run back and tell your dad.'

So Josh came with us down to the dummy grid and we listened to Dad's side of the conversation. 'No, Dad — calm down. Archie's fine. It's a mate of his. Josh. The engine's coughing. No power.' He listened for a couple of steps. 'No. We tried that. It's nothing obvious. Okay. Thanks. Yes, Archie's doing good. Nice and smooth. Okay. Bye.' He gave the phone to Josh. 'He'll have a think and get back to you with an answer.'

Josh trotted off, looking hopeful.

Craig pushed his kart on to pole and ignored me. I was starting on eight, right at the back of the field now that Josh was out — for this race anyway. I was busting to race Craig, to beat him, to make him humble. *Save it for next week. Save it for when it matters. Stick to the game plan.*

The game plan was to try to shave a fraction of a second off every corner. It was to practise my overtaking. To focus on smoothness and consistency.

The starter let us go. There were no surprises. Craig led for the entire race. I let him go and I shaved a hundredth of a second off the S, and another off the left-hander. I went off at the hairpin, but I'd found the limits for it.

I didn't improve my time for the fast lap. That was a worry. It should have been two-hundredths of a second faster. *Try harder next time.*

But Dad said, 'You're shifting your weight slightly in the left-handers. You're not so used to the anti-clockwise track. Could just be the difference.'

'Come off it, Dad. I know not to shift about in the kart.'

'Think about it, Archie. No harm done if I'm wrong.'

Which meant he knew damn well he was right. 'Okay. Did Grandad solve Josh's problem?'

Dad laughed. 'You should have seen Josh's face. He answered the phone, and apparently all the old bugger said was *Bent carby needle* and hung up.'

'And that's what it was?'

He gave me a look. 'What do you think?'

I thought Josh and his dad would be stoked, even if Craig wasn't. Although, scratch that. He'd beaten me again. He'd be very happy.

It nearly killed me to stick to our game plan, but I had work to do. I went into the next race absolutely certain I'd been keeping my body still going into those corners. But this time when we checked the data logger read-out after the race, I'd shaved the time back.

'Okay. You were right,' I said, disgusted with myself for making such a basic mistake.

'You could do with more practice,' Dad said. 'That position needs to be automatic.'

By the time we lined up for the final, I reckoned I had it sorted — I was steady as a statue when I drove those corners.

Because the final grid positions were allocated according to placings in the heats, Craig was on pole and I was on two. I was desperate to beat him, to sneak past, take the lead and keep it. But I thought about next weekend, and I drove to improve, striving for speed, smoothness and consistency. I drove a good race and came in half a kart length behind him.

He wasn't bothered — well, why would he be? He wouldn't have been quite so cocky if he'd known I'd knocked a whole second off my lap times during the day.

He didn't quite strut to the podium back in the clubhouse at prize-giving — not quite. His speech was pure Craig: 'Thank you to the Manawatu Club for an awesome day. I'd like to thank my dad for finding me the best mechanic in the business. Thanks, Gary. And finally a big thank you to Archie Barrington for being such a worthy competitor, as always.'

'That's putting me in my place,' I whispered to Dad.

'He's got balls, all right.'

We were packing up the trailer when Craig came to say goodbye. 'See you next week. Your sponsors will be interested in today's results.'

And off he went, walking cocky, looking cocky, feeling bloody pleased with himself.

Dad said, 'We drive our own race, Archie. Those guys will know what you were doing.'

I hoped so, but Craig was the winner on the day and that's what the sponsors liked.

CHAPTER EIGHT

WE'D BEEN ON the road home for around half an hour before Dad said, 'Happy with the day?'

'Sure am.'

He shifted in the seat, a smile on his face. 'Thought you would be. Craig's happy too.'

I stretched my right arm, flexing the cramping out of it. It ached a bit more than normal thanks to my little encounter with the rocks. But my whole body was sore — it always was after a day's racing. 'I like to make him happy,' I said. Because when he was pumped, he got overconfident, and then he got cocky and that's when he wasn't quite as sharp as he needed to be.

'Got each corner sussed?' Dad asked.

'I reckon. That Two Tree was real mean though. It took me four laps before I found the ideal braking point.'

More kilometres passed in silence. Around Levin, Dad sighed and said, 'Out with it. What's biting you?'

'What if I can't beat him? He's good. He could win the extra sponsorship and the whole Challenge. Or Lewis could.'

'Or somebody else could. Archie, all you can do is your best. Give it everything. If it doesn't work out, you'll know you put your heart out there.'

'Yeah. I know.'

Dad took a hand off the wheel to flick my ear. 'You're a bloody good driver, son. You've got the smarts to win. But things can happen. You know that. So quit thinking about Europe. Stop worrying about nailing the rest of the sponsorship. Take each race as it comes.' This time, he gave me a clip over the head. 'How many times have I told you that?'

'First time this year,' I said. 'I know you're right. I hear you. From now on I'll be Mr Philosophical.' Focus. That's what this year was going to be all about. And staying in the moment.

I spent the time between Porirua and home facing the fact that I mightn't win the chance to race overseas. I looked it square in the eye. I'd never done that before. I'd never truly believed I wouldn't win, that I wouldn't go to Europe. The rest of that dream involved some race team signing me up — but none of it might happen. Bugger it! I didn't want to be philosophical. I wanted to win.

There wouldn't be another chance at the Challenge. We'd decided to go all out for it this year, but that would be it, win or lose. It was too expensive to try again, and Dad seemed to think Year 12 would pile me up with mountains of work and I wouldn't have as much time to put into racing. *You can't set your sights on a career in motor racing* was one of his regular lectures.

We were still ten minutes from home before I turned my mind to the other career that was an option if I really couldn't race. It had sounded good last year when the careers counsellor helped us with our subject choices.

What do you want to do, Archie?

Colin jumped in with: *Formula 1 race driver.*

Ms Arawa ignored him and just kept looking at me, her eyebrows up.

Engineering. I want to design engines.

Colin sat shaking his head. *Mate!*

So this year I was studying subjects that would help me get into engineering at uni. It would be okay. I liked engines and I liked designing things.

I sighed.

Dad said, 'Okay there, son?'

'Yeah.'

He pulled to a stop a street short of our place. 'Listen, Archie. Go out there and have fun. Enjoy it. This is going to be an all-out competitive year. But don't forget that you'll be doing a sport you love. Lose that, and we might as well pack up and stay home.'

I let that sink in. I had an uncomfortable feeling I hadn't taken much notice of that particular lecture before now.

Dad had a range of lectures and I'd taken most of them on board.

Eat well. No problem.

Keep your temper. Again, I'd got that one under control when I was six. I'd got bumped off the track and it wasn't fair. I should have won and I was pretty noisy about it. Dad just said, 'I warned you, Archie. Lose your temper and you lose your kart.' He took it away for three months. Next time, he told me, it'd be for a year.

I made damn sure not to give him any reason to think that I'd forgotten. Strangely, it wasn't a problem now to keep my temper. Win some, lose some. Shrug and drive the next race.

The one lecture that seemed just to have scraped across the surface was the one about handling real, deep disappointment. It went along with the one about accepting that some stuff was going to be out of my control — engine failure, the state of the track, the behaviour of other drivers.

I said, 'Winning's never really mattered before. Not like this. Last year — Craig beat me in the Secondary Schools Champs. I was disappointed but I wasn't gutted.' I stopped to sort out my thoughts.

Dad sat all relaxed, his right arm propped on the steering wheel.

I thumped the dashboard. 'Bugger it, Dad! I want to win this year. I want to be the driver going to Europe.'

'You don't say!' said my father the clown. Then he got serious. 'What's the game plan, then? You need to get your head around the real possibility of failing. *And* you need to drive your heart out.' He started the engine, but left it idling. 'Wednesday,' he said. 'We'll go over your game plan then. And by the way, Erica's at home. She said she'd have dinner ready.'

A game plan by Wednesday, and be nice to Erica and Felix tonight. She'd better be able to cook. My gut was bouncing off my backbone.

As usual, Dad let me sharpen my reversing skills by backing the trailer into the garage when we got home. Erica's Toyota was parked on the road.

He helped me uncouple the trailer and I said, 'Give me a hand with the kart. I'll do the rest. You go in and talk to Erica.' *And get the kissing over with before I come in.*

I STARTED ON the usual post-race routine. I'd taken off the wheels and bodywork, and was unbolting the engine when I felt eyes watching me. Felix, looking scared as usual. He dropped his head and examined the floor the second I noticed him.

Before I even thought what I was doing, I grabbed a rag and threw it to him. 'Catch, Felix. I could do with a hand here. You any good at cleaning?'

He kept his head down but picked up the rag from where it had landed and crept over to the kart.

I pointed at the floor tray. 'Can you have a go at that?'

He dabbed at the mud. It stayed where it was.

Hell. What do you say to a kid as timid as this? Nothing, I decided. I took another rag and rubbed at the nose cone. Felix tilted his head so he could watch me without being obvious about it. After a bit, he put some pressure into the job.

Together, we went over everything. I stood up. 'Good work, buddy. There's still stuff to check, but I reckon we deserve a feed first.'

But Felix stayed squatting on the floor. He didn't say anything, just set to work cleaning the tyres.

'Only the wheels, mate. We don't touch the tyres. But you're right, we should get these done.'

Talk about feeling stupid, cocky, dumb. I was doing it again — taking it for granted that I'd win in the weekend, that I'd beat Craig for the extra sets of tyres and that I'd be the driver going to Europe.

One thing about Felix, he didn't fill your head up with chatter when you needed to think. I needed to think hard. I needed to work out how to keep the dream alive without letting it wreck the entire year. Craig's parting comment about the sponsors hovered in my mind. He was right. They wouldn't be too impressed with the results from today.

Let 'em sweat. I knew what I was doing. To hell with

Craig, too. And Lewis was welcome to try and beat me. Ollie and Josh were in with a chance. Maybe Tama as well. I'd get on the track and fight, just like I always did.

I pulled Felix to his feet. 'One race at a time, Felix, my friend. That's my game plan. Okay, you reckon?'

Poor kid, he looked bewildered. I took the rag from him. 'Thanks, mate. That was a big help.' I flicked my head in the direction of the kitchen. 'Much hugging and kissing going down in there?'

He gave a spluttery sort of giggle.

'Yuck.' I screwed up my face. 'Oh well, I guess we have to face them sooner or later. Don't know about you, but I'm famished. Hungry enough to eat a wheel.'

Erica greeted me with a smile that I translated as *Thank you for being a kind, caring older brother*, but thank god she didn't say anything. She didn't go ape about him being around the kart either. But possibly she hadn't joined those particular dots yet.

She turned out to be a good cook. We had a fancy casserole *and* she'd made a cheesecake.

Dad spoiled the moment by saying, 'You'll need to mow a dozen lawns to work those calories off, Archie.'

'Worth it,' I muttered round a mouthful of my second helping.

'He doesn't need to worry.' She smiled at me. 'Ignore him, Archie. You're young, you're growing and you're lean enough that an extra kilogram or two wouldn't hurt.'

'Power to weight ratios,' Dad said. 'You don't want to be heavier in a kart than the rules say you have to be.'

Erica's face turned to stone. She sent a quick glance in Felix's direction, but he still had his eyes on his plate — not that he'd eaten much.

Oops, Dad — wash your mouth out.

He did a swift direction change. 'But I guess a cheesecake every now and then won't hurt.'

I helped out by saying, 'Could I have another slice, Erica? This leaves those packet ones for dead.'

It looked like we were going to have to be mighty careful about what we said when she was around. And I couldn't see any positives to having Felix around either. Sure, he was quiet. But nobody'd asked me if I wanted to be big brother to a kid who wouldn't utter a word unless it was ripped out of him.

Oh well, I owed him. Thanks to him I had my Wednesday game plan. Just thinking about it made all the usual excitement and sheer fun of racing surge back into my system.

Fighting mongrel with a smart edge, that was me.

CHAPTER NINE

AS ALWAYS AFTER a race weekend, I talked to Grandad before I skyped any of my karting buddies. His weathered face filled my screen. My grandmother leaned over his shoulder.

'How are you, Archie? Good? And that son of ours?'

'Bouncing off the ceiling,' I said. 'Has he told you about Erica?'

They looked at each other, then Grandad said, 'No. But I think we'd rather like to hear about Erica.'

I filled them in, but when Gran tried asking for more details, Grandad shooed her away. 'I've got business to discuss with Archie. Give Bill a call and grill him yourself.'

She waved at me and disappeared. 'Right,' said Grandad. 'Talk me through the day.'

I went over each race, talking tactics and engine set-up. We reviewed the analysis chart we'd done after each race. 'Good. Good,' he said every few minutes. 'And Archie, don't bother bringing food when you come up to Hamilton. Your gran's got it all under control.'

I sat up straighter. 'You'll be there? Cool!'

'We're coming to the whole series, except Manawatu. Got a bloody wedding to go to,' he said. 'But we'll be there for the rest. Have to keep your dad on his toes.'

Yes! I was the third generation of karters in our family, and if the grandparents hadn't taken themselves off to live in Tauranga, Grandad would have made a point of coming to more of my races. He'd taught Dad, the same as Dad was teaching me. I was lucky, I knew that, but on the downside I'd always thought it was me getting into karting that killed Mum and Dad's marriage.

When I'd asked Mum about it, she said, 'It wasn't that, Archie. In the end, we were just too different.' But she'd left when I was six — the year I started karting. Even now, the thought still lurked at the back of my mind that I should have said I didn't want to race.

Erica would probably get fed up too, and walk out. Poor old Dad. The race programme wouldn't be so intense next year but, even so, I didn't want to think about that — about not racing all over the country, or about Dad getting pulled between me and Erica.

I rang Mum next. She asked me about school and I asked her about their organic market garden. Then she surprised me.

'Good luck on the track this year, Archie. Please . . . be careful.'

'Sure, Mum. Course I will. Don't worry.'

But she would worry, and I wouldn't be careful — not in the way she meant, anyway. I was pleased she'd said it, though. She never mentioned my driving if she could help it.

Kyla was my last call. She was on the computer and waiting, a sticking plaster round her left thumb. 'Before you ask,' she said, 'this is the result of an argument with a barbed-wire fence.'

'Ouch. Does it mess up your grip?'

'Not much. Today was a write-off anyway, thanks to

Silver Adams. Honestly, Archie, she's big trouble. A real menace. The stewards had a go at her but it only calmed her down for a couple of races.'

'But she used to be good.' I had a clear memory of a girl with long dark hair, a big laugh and a feel for the kart.

Kyla shook her head. 'She's all thump and bust now. She drives like she wants to clear the track.'

'She'll get herself banned if she's not careful.'

'I don't think they'll ban her. The stewards were pretty lenient with her. People weren't happy about it. But I think there must be a reason. She's changed. She didn't talk to any of us.'

'Well, if you find out anything, let me know. She'll be at Manawatu next weekend, and I could do without having to deal with a crazy driver.'

We talked then about the Nationals coming up at Easter. We'd both be competing, Kyla driving up from Wyndham with her family, and Dad and me taking the ferry to Picton and driving from there.

I took a deep breath. 'We both get there on Thursday, so let's go out that night. Just you and me.'

Her smile beamed from the screen. 'That is a perfect idea.'

DAD LEFT HIS workers to lock up on Wednesday, picked me up from school and drove me to my sponsors to collect the sets of tyres.

Dad shook hands with Brendon and had a man-to-man chat with him. Then Brendon looked at me. 'Craig did well on Sunday.'

'Yes. He's a good driver,' I said. 'Beating him wasn't my aim, though.'

'We expect you to *race* for us, Archie.'

'I've shaved my times on every corner, thanks to Sunday.' I didn't say anything else, just left it there for him to think about.

It took him two seconds. 'I hear you. Good man.'

They loaded the tyres into the van, handshakes all round, and we were off. Dad was chuckling away to himself. 'I've never seen light dawn on a man's face like it did with him. Well done, Archie.' Then, without a pause, he said, 'Have you got that game plan worked out yet?'

'Yeah. It's simple — I take each race as it comes. Race my guts out. Never forget how much I love the speed and the excitement.'

'That'll do it,' said my father. 'And by the way, we're both having dinner at Erica's tonight.'

'I'll take my homework with me. That way I won't have to watch the love birds.' And I wouldn't get stuck with Felix either.

We went, we ate, we enjoyed. Felix didn't utter a word. I finished a science assignment, zapped through the maths and we went home at 9.30.

'Erica worries about Felix,' Dad said.

'And you've told her karting would bring him out of his shell?'

He gave me a look. 'I'm not that stupid. She's about as keen on it as Gracie is.' Gracie being my mother.

'It would though,' I said.

'I know. But there it is. Don't suggest it, Archie. I don't want to scare her off.'

I patted his knee. 'Don't worry, old man. I'll be a good boy.'

He clipped my ear for me and I laughed. I was getting used to the Erica/Felix idea. Sure, life would change but some of the changes were looking as though they'd be positive. I hadn't been so deep in my homework that I hadn't heard Erica telling Dad that, if he didn't mind, she'd like to cook at least three nights a week. I could cope with that.

I TURNED UP at school on Thursday with my mind on the next three days.

'Earth to Archie,' Ginnie said, waving her hand in front of my face.

'We're coming to watch you on Sunday,' Colin said.

'All of you?'

'They've bullied us into it,' Nina said.

'What time do we need to be there?' Colin asked.

'Seven thirty,' I said.

He was surprised. 'Night racing? Hell. I don't think Mum'll be up for that.'

'Seven thirty in the morning.'

The others spluttered with laughter but shook their heads. 'No way. We'd have to leave here about five.'

'Five in the morning is not a time that exists as far as I'm concerned,' Ginnie said.

'My heat is 10.30.' I ducked out of the way of Colin's fist.

Ginnie was still looking unhappy. 'Jeez, that means we'll have to leave here about 8.30.' She rolled her eyes. 'The things I do in the name of friendship.'

'You could just come for the pre-final and the final, if

you want,' I told them. 'They're in the afternoon.'

'Let me get my head around this,' Silas said. 'You have one heat, then the pre-final and then the final?'

'You got it. We do the practising tomorrow. Saturday is the qualifying rounds. Fastest time gets pole position for the two heats. They run the first heat on Saturday.' Just talking about it sent the shivers of excitement through me.

'And you want pole,' Nina said. The girls looked at each other. 'That's three races. Those karts stink and they're hell loud. I say we arrive in time for the final.'

'Girls!' said Colin. 'Wear earplugs. We'll go all day.'

I let them squabble. I wouldn't have time to hang out with them, but it'd be great to have them there, cheering for me.

'Archie, what do you think?' Nina asked. 'Seen one, seen them all? Just watching the final — that'll be all right, won't it?'

'Yeah. It's just like rugby. Seen one test match, seen them all.' She was the hugest rugby fan.

She bunted me with her shoulder. 'It so is not!'

'You don't know,' Colin said. 'You've never watched a race. How about we go for the afternoon? Mum's driving, and she won't be keen on staying the whole day anyway.'

'But then we'll only be able to watch the final,' Silas said. 'What's the point?'

'There's the pre-final too,' I said. 'It's worth winning that, because then you get pole position on the grid for the final.'

'Do you want us to come?' Nina asked. 'Will it make any difference?'

It wouldn't make any difference — I wouldn't be able

to hear them cheering and I'd be too busy driving to look at them. 'It'd be cool to have you there. Yeah, I'd like to have a fan zone.' Craig's mates often came to cheer him when we raced in Auckland. He didn't seem to have girl friends — it was always just guys who turned up.

'I say we go for the afternoon,' James said. 'We watch the pre-final and the final. Okay?'

And so it was decided.

'Cool,' I said. 'Thanks, guys.'

At home that evening I checked the entry list. Twenty-six in my class. That was good, although we probably wouldn't finish the year with that many. I scanned the names. No surprises until I got to Sel. Couldn't believe it — he must've won Lotto.

I texted him: *U entering the challenge? No bullshit?*

C u tomorrow. Thanx 2 my sponsor.

Who?

Gran.

I laughed and texted back: *Cool*

Time for bed. I was almost asleep when a text arrived from Kyla: *Drunk driver killed silvers mum xmas eve.*

I stared at it. That was only a couple of months ago. I texted back: *That wld explain it. Jeez.*

CHAPTER TEN

ON FRIDAY MORNING Silver's dad set up their base three away from ours. Silver came out of the tent and stood looking over the track.

Dad said, 'Go and tell her you're sorry about her mother.'

'I'm not doing that! She probably doesn't even remember me.'

He put down the spanner and gave me one of his looks.

'What?'

'Two things. First, it's the decent thing to do . . .'

'You do it then.'

'And second, if you don't, it's going to be the elephant in the room all year. The thing nobody talks about. And soon it'll turn into the thing nobody *can* talk about.' He gave me a nod and went back to what he'd been doing. Bloody hell, I hated that — he'd tell me something I didn't want to hear, then leave me alone to come around to his way of thinking.

There'd been a few times at school . . . Girls had it easy — they just went straight into the hug, let loose some tears and then we could all talk.

'Craig's going over to her now,' I said, and shot out of the tent. He'd say something, and I could just nod and look sorry. But he stopped a metre short and didn't even glance at her.

Shit. I was there now, stuck between her and Craig. 'Uh, hi, Silver. Listen, I heard about your mum. I'm really sorry.'

She turned, flicked her eyes over me and slouched off.

Thanks, Dad.

'The word is we need to watch out for her on the track,' Craig said.

'Did you hear what happened to her mother?'

'Yes, I heard. So what? That's her private life. It's got nothing to do with racing.'

Correct, but hard. I went back to Dad, who asked, 'How did it go?'

'Let's just say I won't be mentioning her mum again any time soon.'

'You did the right thing, son.' He gave me a shoulder squeeze.

I put Silver out of my mind. It was scrutineering time.

We wheeled the kart down to the tech shed and joined the queue behind Tama. There were seven in front of him.

Our turn. The official checked my race gear and all the paperwork. Next came the drivers' briefing, and I don't reckon I imagined it but the stewards seemed to be stressing the good-driving message. A couple of guys looked at Silver. I was behind her and slightly to the side, but as far as I could tell she ignored them and the official doing the briefing.

The rest of the day had its usual dramas. My kart threw a chain. Jack spent more time on the grass than on the black stuff. Ollie missed most of the morning's practice because his engine wouldn't start. By the time we were ready to pack up, though, I was feeling ready for tomorrow's qualifiers and the heat.

Back at the motel, we went to bed early. The next two days would be big.

⊙

I WOKE IN the morning to a day of clear sunshine. It was going to get hot. We drove to the track behind Craig and his new mechanic. I wondered if Craig had been watching for us, just to make sure he led the way. He'd be hoping to score a psychological point.

He made sure he was first, too, when we lined up for our initial qualifier. It was all part of his game plan — be first even when it didn't matter. In the qualifiers all that mattered was keeping clear of everyone else so you could clock up the fastest lap time. I guessed he was trying to make us all believe he deserved to be out in front and therefore we wouldn't go all out to beat him. Like that was going to work.

He'd be missing out on pole this time, though. Josh and his dad were already halfway there.

Craig positioned his kart on two, grinned at Josh and said something I didn't catch, but it made Josh laugh.

Silver put her kart on three. Dad said, 'You want four? It'd keep you out of her way.'

'Nah. Ten's about where I'd like to be.' I figured it was better to work out how to beat Silver Adams now when it didn't matter so much. Besides, I wasn't going to let her scare me into playing it safe.

When we were all positioned, there were twenty-six

karts on the grid. Most of us were competing in the Challenge and every single one of us was desperate to win the prize of racing in Europe at the end of the year. Except maybe Silver.

Realistically, there were five of us with a chance: Craig, Ollie, Lewis, Josh and me. Sel might, but he was an outside chance.

I pulled on my helmet, slipped into my kart and settled myself to wait out the long minutes before the starter released us from the dummy grid out on to the track. I didn't mind the wait. None of us did. It meant we could still our minds, focus on the race ahead, run the track through the mental video, and all the time we were shut off, secure in our own worlds.

The starter gave the signal. His hand dropped and we were off, each of us doing our own thing. I turned the steering wheel sharply a few times in a zigzag to scuff in my new tyres. I planned on taking it easy for the first two laps until my tyres warmed up, but even so I slipped past Julian Chub when his kart took seconds to build up power again after braking.

I stayed tucked in behind Sel but let the space between us lengthen. Up ahead, Angus love-tapped the back of Silver's kart, letting her know he was there, that he wanted to pass. She altered her line to block him. Not strictly illegal.

I checked the engine temp on the data logger. It was running a touch hot. Not surprising. The day was going to be a scorcher. I flipped up the radiator cover. The kart felt good.

I drove without thinking about it, watching ahead, keeping out of trouble and checking the timing each time I completed a lap. I was still a whole second slower than my best lap from club day.

Up ahead, Sel was closing in on 47 — Silver's kart. She aimed at the corner, Sel on her tail. Braked too late and spun off on to the paddock. Sel got sucked into the spin and followed her.

I kept my eyes on the track ahead and avoided the carnage.

Lap five and I had clear track ahead of me. I checked the data logger. Craig would waltz on to pole if I couldn't do better than I'd managed so far.

With Josh, Ollie and Craig well out of the way ahead of me, I settled in for some serious driving. It was time to push, to drive to the limit. Fastest lap time and pole position. That was what I was after.

Smoothness, speed and judgement. Every brain cell firing. Every nerve alert.

The chequered flag, and impossible to tell who'd clocked the fastest time. I was happy, though. Everything felt good. The kart was responsive and the engine singing. I checked the data logger, then switched it off. A clear half second faster than my best lap the weekend before.

Back in the pits, Craig asked, 'What's your time?'

I pulled a face. 'Not enough.' I gave him the time, but I added a second. I didn't ask him what his was. No point. He wouldn't tell me the truth either.

'What d'you think?' Dad asked as he helped me lift the kart on to the trolley. 'Everything okay?'

'Spot on,' I said. 'We don't need to change a thing.'

Back in the tent, he said, 'Archie, you're going to have to watch out for Silver. She's clever. She's not blatant enough for the stewards to haul her up, but she's blocking and barging and keeping just inside the rule book.'

'She hasn't driven for a couple of years. I should be able to get past her.' Easy enough to get behind her at the hairpin and duck through. 'Did you talk to her old man?'

Dad looked offended. 'Of course I did. We had quite a chat. He said Silver's taken it hard. That's why he bought her the kart — to give her something positive to do.'

'Does he call making a nuisance of herself positive?'

'Yes, Archie, he does. He knows what she's doing and he's talked to her about it. But he isn't going to try to stop her. He's just grateful she's racing.'

She wouldn't be as fast as I was, so she'd be behind me on the grid. I wasn't bothered about Silver Adams.

'Grid positions are up.' Craig stuck his head into our tent. 'You interested in checking them out?'

We collected Josh, Ollie, Lewis and Sel on the way. Silver stood outside her base, staring at the ground. I could practically hear Dad's voice in my head: *Do the decent thing, Archie.* So I said, 'You coming, Silver?'

She didn't move, and she kept her mouth shut.

'Forget her,' Craig said, loud enough for her to hear.

Josh ran ahead, desperate to find his position. 'I'm on five! Yes!'

Craig walked faster. I let him go. I'd find out soon enough. He took a quick scan of the board, then threw up his arms. 'There's been a mistake! Archie's on pole! Noooo!'

But despite the clowning, he was right pissed off. He shook his head, looking disgusted now. 'One lousy tenth of a bleeding second. But I will get my revenge, my friend. Those last three sets of slicks are mine for the taking.'

Interesting. I'd forgotten about the tyres.

There's nothing like pushing your kart on to pole position. The heat started, and I banished Craig from my mind. He was right behind me, but it was my race now. I flew into each corner, not thinking about the driving — just doing it. The laps counted down. The field spread out behind me. Lap six the engine was running hot. I flipped open the radiator cover to get some air through. My lap times were good. Craig was right there, always behind me, always looking to overtake. *I'll show you, you prick!*

Big mistake. I flew into the right-hander on the second to last lap, left the braking a fraction too late and ended up on the grass. This time I didn't waste time beating myself up. Not yet. It was back on the track, go like shit, make up lost time.

I finished eighth. Could have been worse. Should have been a hell of a lot better.

'How did that happen?' Dad asked when we were back at our base.

'Thinking about beating Craig. Took my mind off my own race.' I was totally disgusted with myself.

Dad just shook his head. 'Lucky for you Grandad isn't here.'

Yeah. He tended to go ballistic. Maybe that was why Dad did the opposite and left it to me work out how stupid I'd been. 'I won't bloody do it again.'

Lucky for me, my little picnic on the grass wouldn't affect my grid position for the second heat. We kept the same positions for both heats.

Dad didn't mention it again but he didn't have to. I went over and over my mistake all the way back to the motel. Before we got out of the van, he said, 'Keep your mind on the next heat. Learn from that mistake and make bloody sure you don't get caught like that again.'

I wasn't looking forward to my de-brief with Grandad, though. In the end, I put the phone down on the table, picking it up again only once he'd run out of steam. He finished by saying, 'Keep your mind on the job, Archie. Get a good sleep tonight.'

Dad gave me a grin. 'I guess you got the message?'

'Loud and clear.'

I went to bed, focusing my thoughts on the day ahead.

CHAPTER ELEVEN

SUNDAY WAS ANOTHER scorcher. It was a day for wearing swimming togs rather than kitting up in race gear. Would I have swapped? Not on your life.

Our heat was called. I used the waiting time on the grid to still my mind, to clear it of everything except the track, the race and my tactics. I visualised the start. Craig would try to cut across me to grab the inside.

Breathe. Relax. Focus.

I was ready. The starter let us go. Round we went in formation. The lights went out.

Craig jumped the start. Not by much, and not enough for the stewards to get excited, but he accelerated early enough to cut me off and take the lead.

I'd think about it later. Right now, I had a job to do and that was to get past him, stay on the track and stay legal.

I chased him, right on his tail, for an entire lap — just letting him know I was there. The next lap, I snuck past him at Two Tree. Yay for last week's practising. The race was now mine. All I had to do was be consistent, be fast and stay on the track. Every corner, he was there, tapping the rear of my kart. Every straight, he popped out from my slipstream. But I had the inside and he had to fall back in the corners.

The final lap. He was there beside me again, moving

his body backwards and forwards, urging more speed from his engine. I held myself still and just drove.

We hurtled the final few metres side by side. Had I won? I didn't know. We circled back round the track, slowing to leave at the pit exit.

'Not bad,' Dad said.

'Who won?'

'You. By three-hundredths. How come he beat you off the start?'

I shrugged, but once we were back in our tent, I said, 'The prick jumped the start.'

Dad looked thoughtful. 'He's out to win then. He won't be happy you got past him. Put him out of your mind, Archie. We drive our own race.'

We ate lunch, then started going over the kart, tightening and checking everything. Our heads were down in the engine when my mates arrived.

'Archie! We made it. You wouldn't believe the drama we had finding the bloody place.' They crowded round us, laughing and chattering.

Dad glanced up and caught my eye. I said, 'Great to see you, guys. How about I give you the grand tour?'

'Put your suit on properly,' Ginnie said. 'You're making the place untidy.'

'You're not the only one.' Silas looked around. Everybody in a racing suit had it unzipped and pulled down to waist level.

'It's hot,' I said. 'Come on, I'll show you round.'

I did my best with the guide duties but my mind was on the track.

'You won't be on pole for the pre-final then?' Ginnie asked after I told them about the heats. She sounded disappointed.

I pointed at the notice board. 'That guy's putting the positions up now. Let's go have a look-see.'

Silver wandered along ahead of us, head down as always. Anna, the only other girl in the race, was beside her. They didn't talk to each other.

'Four,' I said. 'Could have been worse.'

Craig, as expected, had pole. A win and a second in the heats — he was always going to be on pole for the pre-final. Ollie was on two and Sel was beside me on three. Josh was behind us on five. Thanks to a picnic on the grass, Lewis was back on seven.

When we'd moved away from the notice board, I filled my mates in about who to watch for. 'Craig's the main opposition.'

'Archie's got an arch-rival,' said Colin.

'Sorry, old man,' I said, 'but that's not the first time that joke's been given an outing.'

'We'll boo him for you,' Nina said. 'Put a hex on his wheels.'

'Keep an eye on Silver for me, will you? Kart 47. She's the rogue in the pack.' I gave them a brief explanation.

'Sounds like she's taking her anger out on the track,' Nina said.

'Yeah, but I don't want to be her punching bag,' I said. I showed them a good position to watch from, and left them to it.

'Everything okay?' I asked when I got back to base.

'Spot on,' Dad said. 'And Grandad says text him after the final. Quote: *I'll be in the bloody church watching a bloody wedding. Need something to stop me puking.* So don't make him yell instead.'

'I'll do my best,' I said.

CHAPTER TWELVE

THE PRE-FINAL STARTED with no drama. No changes in position for the first lap and a half, then I got past Sel as we came out of the bend on to the back straight. Only Ollie and Craig to pick off now. I followed them through the tight section of the track, planning on sneaking past Ollie on the hairpin, but he had Craig in his sights. He braked early and lost time at the exit. I slipped under and through, and was off after Craig, hunting him down.

He'd be expecting somebody to have a go at him. He'd be alert and watchful.

I was right there on his tail as we drove the tight part of the track. I'd have been faster round Two Trees if he hadn't been in my way. The hairpin was up ahead. Yes! I outbraked him and snuck through but, when I eased the power back on, the full kick wasn't there and he took the lead again.

Bugger it, what was wrong? It wasn't much — just enough to slow me down a fraction getting back up to full revs. Ollie passed me on the next bend, with Lewis right behind him. I managed to hold off Josh and the guy in Kart 42 but only by a whisker.

Fourth again. Could have been worse, and at least this one wasn't my fault.

'What's wrong?' Dad asked.

'Not enough power coming out of the corners.'

We took the kart back to our base. I'd forgotten about my friends, but they arrived in a chattering, excited bunch, firing questions at full throttle.

'Archie. Scram,' said Dad.

I didn't want to go, but knew he'd do better without me anyway.

'So — that Silver,' Ginnie said. 'This kart was right behind her. She swung out to let him pass her, but then she changed her mind and went back.'

'Bumped him right off the track,' Silas said. 'Awesome crash.'

'The guy behind got the next kart up his rear end and the two of them spun out as well.' James rubbed his face as if he couldn't quite believe it. 'Man, the racing's fast. I hadn't realised.' He looked at me with a mix of respect and surprise.

I let their talk swirl around me. Keep well away from Silver — that would be the good idea of the year.

They went back to the grandstand to watch the seniors. I left them to it.

Dad had my kart outside with the engine running, his head tilted, listening. He reached in and switched it off. 'Sounds okay now. I adjusted the jetting. Let's hope that's all it was.'

I HAD MY work cut out if I wanted to win the final. Number four on the grid, with three good drivers to get past. I pulled on my helmet, got into my seat and settled myself into my prep.

My start was good. I cut across Lewis to pull ahead of him up the straight. Just Ollie and Craig to pick off.

Ollie helped me out by going wide on Clubhouse Corner. I got through, closing in on Craig, letting him know I was there, that I was after him, aiming to unsettle him.

But he was good.

We went smoothly into the right-hand bend. He drove a perfect line. He had that corner nailed, leaving the braking till the last second. I knew he would. I braked early, changing my line through the corner to duck in under him. I was past! The revs built up to full throttle, giving me full power.

I was leading with seven laps still to go. *Consistent, Archie. Go for smoothness and consistency.*

Time after time I roared over the start/finish line, counting down the laps. Craig appeared on the straights, popping up on the edges of my vision. I drove my own race, not hard out but going at around eighty per cent capacity until the final two laps. Ninety per cent, that's what I wanted — just pushing that little bit harder, hitting my braking points closer to the outside limits.

I forgot about Craig. I was in the zone, actions on automatic, in a world apart.

Final lap. Right-hander at the end of the straight, another straight, another right-hander. I held the kart steady. No need to get smart, no need to prove anything. Just keep driving.

The chequered flag, Craig edging up beside me too late. I was over the line, fractions of a second ahead of him. I slowed down, cruising back to the pits, a grin on my face and satisfaction oozing through every pore of my body. I'd done it.

I stayed with the kart while it was checked for compliance. Dad was waiting for me when I came back.

'Kart okay, then?'

'Perfect. Thanks, Dad.'

He held out his phone. Grandad's text read: *V g*

'Short and to the point,' said Dad. 'He'll be right stoked.'

My friends arrived in a noisy whirl. 'That was *amazing*!'

'You're the man, Archie!'

'We hexed him good!'

'That number 19, he's going to be so gutted.' Craig was 19. He wouldn't be gutted, though. He'd be furious, and probably taking it out on poor old Gary.

'What happens now?' James asked.

'We hang about for a bit. Then it's prize-giving.'

'That's worth staying for,' said my helpful father. 'Always enlightening listening to what Archie has to say.'

Which naturally had the effect of making them determined to hang around just to listen to my fabulous oratory.

I did my best not to disappoint them, or Craig. 'First of all,' I said, 'I want to thank my fantastic sponsors.' And I did a bit of a rave about the tyres. 'Thanks as always to Dad, and to my grandad who was our remote mechanic. Lastly, thanks as ever to Craig Bateman for being such a worthy competitor.'

That was probably mean. Couldn't resist it, though. I'd just have to make bloody sure I didn't let him beat me for the rest of the year.

As we were packing up, Craig — who never did any packing except to help lift his kart into the trailer — strolled up. 'Enjoy the win while you can, mate. It's the only one you're going to get this year.'

I grinned at him. 'Been reading the fortune cookies again, have you?'

He laughed and took himself off. It was a long wait till the next big event when we'd race each other again. That would be in Christchurch at the Nationals over Easter.

On the way home, I got a text from my sponsors. *Congrats Archie. Well done. Write us an article for the website pls.*

I read it out to Dad. 'Shit. They didn't say anything about that!'

'Good experience,' said my father. 'You might end up as a sports journalist.'

Yeah, right. I wasn't that fond of writing, but most of all, I'd hate to just be watching when I could be out there in the middle of the action.

CHAPTER THIRTEEN

'DON'T FORGET ERICA'S moving in next weekend,' Dad said as we neared home.

It turned out there was small chance of being allowed to forget that, what with all the extra cleaning we apparently needed to do, and no handy thunderbolt hurtling down from the sky bawling at Dad that this was a bad idea. He wouldn't have heard anyway, the way he bounced around with a goofy grin on his face all that week. And he kept singing. My feeling is that if you want to sing, but basically you can't, then you should only do it where you can't be heard.

I wrote the piece for the sponsor's blog, and recycled it for English. Colin suggested that it'd be a good idea to write his assignment as well.

'A good idea for who?'

'Not you,' Nina said, shoving him. 'Miss would know straight up that you didn't write it.'

'We could all do ours about going and watching though,' Ginnie said.

When we got them back, I'd got a merit, Silas an excellence and the others managed an achieved. Colin was stoked.

February morphed into March

The great moving day arrived, Erica all bustle and

energy, with Felix shuffling along behind looking miserable. Poor kid, a good blat in a kart would be so brilliant for him. I couldn't stand it.

'I'm off to the park to do some training. Felix, you wanna come and help?'

He didn't say a word, just scuttled over to the door and slid out in front of me. I shut it while Erica was doing a witter about being careful.

We walked and Felix was his usual chatty self, so to fill in the silence I gave him Dad's *keep fit/keep strong* lecture. He might have been interested, but equally he could have been bored out of his skull. Had to be better than being fussed over by his mother, though.

We got to the park. No play equipment. Bugger, I hadn't thought about that. I couldn't leave the poor kid standing on the side watching me run.

'Hey, Felix — I'm going to do some laps. You start running, just jogging so that I go faster. Then when I catch you up, I've got to carry you for twenty steps. Weight training. Okay?'

He gave a tiny nod and I reckon there was almost a grin. So I ran, and so did he, the little rat — I really had to chase him. 'Got you!' I swung him over my shoulder, ran for twenty, then set him down.

But he grabbed hold of my shirt. 'Nineteen. You only did nineteen.'

'Twenty. That was a big fat twenty.'

We kept jogging with him dragging on my shirt.

'Nineteen.'

I scooped him up under one arm, took a huge stride, then tumbled him on to the ground. 'Twenty-one!' I took off, and this time he cut across the park so that he was running behind me with the idea of making me do another full lap before I caught him. I pivoted, grabbed and tipped him upside down, running with his head just clear of my knees. 'Nineteen, twenty, twenty-one!'

We stayed in the park for ages, clowning around, getting crazier and crazier until we ended up rolling on the grass, laughing our sides sore.

There was a real person inside that kid. Who knew?

As we strolled home, I said, 'You're a bit grubby, mate.'

'Yes,' he said, and smiled a proper, full stretch of the lips.

Erica didn't make a fuss. She was surprised, though, no doubt about it.

I looked around the lounge. 'Wow. This looks . . . different.'

'Good different or bad different?' She sounded worried.

I shook my head. 'Just . . . different. It'll take a bit of getting used to. I don't hate it.'

'That's a good start.'

I wondered what she'd done with our old thin cushions. And had she bought that rug especially to cover up the baked-bean stain on the carpet?

'Nice painting.' I walked over to get a closer look. Hills, sky, autumn colours, bold strokes. The artist's signature was in the corner. *Erica*. 'You painted it?'

'It's my hobby — I'm nothing special, but I'm pleased you like it.'

I liked the meal she'd brought with her too. Life, it seemed, would chug along.

EASTER, AND THE National Champs in Christchurch, got closer. I worked on my kart every spare moment I had, cleaning it, checking for cracks, making sure no bolts were missing and there were no worn parts on any of the nuts or bolts. I greased and lubed the bearings.

Dad put in the hours whenever Erica was on duty. It had taken me a few days to get around to asking what sort of doctoring she did. I expected her to say she did kids' stuff, from what Dad had said earlier about getting upset when they got hurt, but no, she worked in Casualty. 'And I don't want to see you being brought in on a stretcher, Archie.' That was the nearest she got to saying outright what she thought about my racing. My private hope that we would be able to get Felix into a kart curled up and died.

Thursday a week before Easter, Dad and Erica planned a night out — dinner and a show. Wednesday night, Felix's carer rang to say she couldn't look after him the following night after all. Erica went into a 360. It was all *Oh my god, what'll I do?*

Dad gave me a look. Felix, saying nothing as always, studied the floor.

I shrugged. 'He can stay here,' I said. 'I'm not going anywhere.'

Erica shook her head. 'Definitely not. I promised Bill I wouldn't take advantage of either of you. I'll sort it out. Don't worry.'

I rolled my eyes at Dad, and said to Felix, 'Come on, mate. We'll leave them to argue it out.' I went through to the garage, Felix hard on my heels.

Dad won. Felix stayed with me and helped me cook us a feed. I'd planned on spending the evening watching karting DVDs, then doing a bit of skyping. So that's what I did, and if Felix was dead keen to watch with me — well, I couldn't help that.

'We've seen that one two times,' he said.

'Yeah. Sorry about that, but that's what I do. You don't have to watch, though. Grab a book. Or a puzzle.'

He stayed glued to the sofa. 'Why?'

'Why do I watch it over and over?'

A nod.

'That guy — in number 90 — he's one of the best. I'm trying to learn from him. See how he got past that other kart? That's pure skill. His kart's not faster, or better. But he gets past because he's a better driver than anyone else on the track.'

I talked Felix through it. 'They're both coming up to the corner now. Number 90 brakes just fractionally later. Then he ducks under and through. That way you don't waste time. It's all about timing, mate. All about trying to be faster than the other guy.'

It wasn't a bad evening. I even read him a chapter of the story he and Erica were partway through. 'You're going to have to do without the goodnight kiss,' I told him. 'I'm saving those for my girlfriend.'

I heard him giggling as I left the room. I'd be seeing Kyla in a week. Dinner out. Just the two of us. Dad owed me — and he'd better not try any smart comments either. Not after all the lovey dovey grief he and Erica treated me and the kid to.

CHAPTER FOURTEEN

DAD AND I were deep in kart prep over the next week, and we weren't as careful as we'd been up till then to keep it all low key when Erica was around. Like when we went over the analysis charts, and there was Felix sitting on the other side of the table, drinking in every word.

Tuesday morning at breakfast, Dad said, 'Check the trailer inventory tonight, Archie. If we're short of anything, I can get it tomorrow.'

I'd pack my gear as well, running through our checklist to make sure I had all the paperwork, helmet, rib protectors, suit, gloves. The works.

Erica suddenly got very busy packing Felix off to school.

School had that end-of-term feel about it. Mr Taylor reminded us rather tetchily that we still had two more days until the Easter holiday, so buckle down, shut up and work.

'Some of us only have one day,' Colin said, and not in a whisper either.

Mr Taylor ignored him. Dad had already got permission for me to skip Thursday. When the bell rang, Mr T said, 'Good luck, Archie.'

Colin jabbed my ribs with his elbow. 'You'd fall into shit and come up smelling of roses.'

'It's my winning personality,' I said.

James said, 'Make sure you beat that Craig guy. He was a bit too up himself, I reckon.'

'Good-looking, though,' Ginnie said.

'And rolling in the dollars,' Nina said.

Girls! I wondered what Kyla thought of him. Maybe it'd be safer not to ask.

I waved goodbye to my mates and rode home. A couple of streets away from my house I spotted Felix jogging along with a determined look on his face. I cruised up beside him and dismounted.

'What's up, buddy?'

He stopped, and — surprise, surprise, he looked square at me. 'I want to help.'

I joined a few dots. 'With the kart?'

He nodded and, man, did he look stubborn. Not my fight. I pulled out my phone, hit Erica's number and held it out to him. 'Argue it out with your mum.'

His end of the conversation was pretty much a blank. I wasn't surprised when he gave the phone to me — without saying anything, naturally. I took it and damn near dropped it. She was going ballistic. 'Archie, I will not tolerate this sneaking around. You might be obsessed with speed, but I'm not having that for my son. I respect that it's important to you, and I don't think it's asking too much for you to respect what's important to me.'

Bugger you, lady. 'Sure. Next time I see Felix walking along the road all on his lonesome, I'll just ride on and ignore him. Fine.' I hung up on her.

Felix stuck his hands behind his back. 'I want to help.'

I wanted to ride off and leave him, but it wasn't his fault he had a psycho for a mother. I started walking at his speed towards home. No way was I going to do her dirty work. If she wanted Felix to be somewhere he didn't want to be, it was her problem. Not mine.

He came along too.

My phone rang. 'What?'

'I'm sorry. I apologise. I jumped to conclusions. His carer was on her way to his school to find out where he was. Would you mind taking him back to her?'

The bloody nerve of her! 'I'm not doing that. I've got work to do. He doesn't want to go and I'm not carrying a yelling kid down the street. He can come with me.'

I turned the phone off, and we walked home in silence. I made us a drink and a sandwich.

'Are you mad at me?' he asked.

Jeez, more words from the kid than I'd heard him speak in his life. 'No. I'm plenty mad at your mum though.'

'Can I still help?'

'Absolutely.'

I gave him the check sheet. 'Call out each thing on here. If I say *okay*, you cross it out. And don't miss a single thing or I could be up shit creek without a paddle.'

He struggled with some of the words, but we got it done and I made out a list for Dad. All we had to get was more two-stroke oil and a chain.

'Thanks, mate,' I said. 'Your reward for helping is to be assistant chef.'

'I can peel potatoes.'

'You're the man. Spud duty for you.'

By the time Dad and Erica arrived home, the two of

us were setting the table. Felix threw me the cutlery and I put it in place.

Felix looked at his mother. 'I helped.'

She came over all emotional, gave him a hug and a kiss. Dad gave me a very sneaky thumbs-up.

WE DIDN'T TALK about the Felix incident until we were on the ferry bright and disgustingly early the next morning.

'What happened?' Dad asked.

I told him everything, including the spaz from his girlfriend. I was still mad at her.

'You did well, Archie.' He patted my shoulder. 'She's thrilled with how much Felix has come out of his shell. It's mainly due to you, and she knows it.'

'She's got a damn strange way of being thrilled.'

'Go easy on her, son. She's had to patch up enough accident victims to know what can happen.'

I shook my head. 'It's still a mystery how you two ever got together.' I didn't mean that exactly. I knew how they'd met — Dad had to collect somebody for his work from the airport. The plane was two hours late, he had a coffee, Erica asked to share his table because all the others were full. They talked. The time flew. And now she was living in my house.

'Some things are just meant to happen,' said Dad, getting all dreamy eyed.

I pulled out my phone and started a text chat with Kyla.

We got to Christchurch late afternoon. Dad parked

the trailer and I went to have a look over the track before it closed for the day. I walked past trailers I recognised — Craig's for starters. Silver's was there too, beside Sel. Next to him was somebody I didn't recognise, then Jack and Tama. Kyla's was across from ours. Good, she was here already.

A couple of karts were out on the track, practising. I watched them, taking note of the cornering. The driver in 38 needed to keep his head still — it waved all over the place.

I'd be out there tomorrow. It was too late now to get in any decent practice.

Kyla and her family were in the motel unit next to ours. It took about half an hour before the two of us could get away.

'Back home by eight,' Dad shouted after us.

'Nine,' I said to Kyla.

She tucked her hand in mine and we left the rellies behind. We jumped on a bus and hit the town. It was hard to remember how it had been before the quakes, everything had changed so much. We wandered around, not worrying about where we were going. I put my arm around Kyla. It felt good to be walking with my girl.

We got hungry. 'Good healthy food. Or pizza?'

But neither of us wanted to compromise our fitness. 'Let's do both,' she said.

What a girl! We had salads, followed by woodfired pizza.

When I got back to the motel — at nine — Dad said, 'Good time?'

'Yep.'

I didn't tell him how we'd walked by the river. I didn't

tell him how we'd kissed. There are some things a father doesn't need to know.

'Craig popped in for a chat. He wanted to know where you were.'

'What did you tell him?'

'That you were out at the track. You've never seen a guy vanish so quick.'

CHAPTER FIFTEEN

NEXT MORNING, WE were all at the track as soon as it opened. Craig just happened to mention that he had a new engine. 'It's fast. Dad bought it off Phil Karaka.' Phil Karaka used to be the fastest guy in our class, but he needed a different type of engine now that he'd got too heavy and had to move up to the seniors.

'I hope Phil charged him double the cost of a new one,' I said to Kyla.

Dad laughed when I told him. 'You can have the fastest engine on the track, but if you haven't got the best driver and the best set-up, you might as well save your money.'

The practice runs had more than their usual dramas, thanks to Craig and Silver. She got to the grid before he did for the first run, and took pole. Josh was right behind her and pushed his kart on to two. Ollie and Jack bagged three and four, and Craig had to be satisfied with five, beside Lewis on six. I put my kart on fifteen, happy to be well away from Silver. Craig, though, would want to be in front — all part of his psychological game-playing. But it wasn't so smart to set himself up for a tangle with Silver, in my opinion.

I made sure I stayed well away from the pair of them and settled in for some serious driving. Fastest lap time was what I wanted. Me and every other driver.

Don't think about them. Don't think. Just drive.

I passed when I had to, but mostly I was able to maintain enough distance from the karts in front of me so that I could concentrate on shaving fractions of seconds off my time in each corner.

By the time the session finished, I was happy. Craig and any other bugger would have to drive bloody well to beat me.

'All okay?' Dad asked when he met me at the pits.

'Spot on.'

We waited for Kyla, then took the karts back to our bases. She looked pleased with her time but neither of us bothered asking the other what we'd clocked.

'Craig's not going to be happy,' Dad said when we were in our tent. 'Silver managed to block him for an entire lap. Looked to me like he was so mad he lost his focus after that. Didn't put in even one decent lap.'

'A pity he gets another chance,' I said. I wasn't worried.

But I wasn't the only one trying not to laugh too loudly when they called our second practice. There was old Silver on pole, standing beside her kart and staring out at nothing. Craig let go his trolley and strode over to her, waving his hands and jabbing at the air. Kyla and I were too far away to hear, but we could guess. Craig yelled. Silver kept staring at nothing — it looked like she wasn't even aware of him.

A steward tapped Craig on the shoulder, said something, then pointed at the back of the grid. Gary the mechanic, his face very grim, took it on himself to push Craig's kart on to number twenty-four. That wasn't Craig's favourite position.

Kyla and I chose spots in the middle of the field — it looked like being a good idea to keep out of the way of both of them. I wondered what my sponsors would think of Craig's meltdown. Their problem, not mine. I'd use the session to perfect each corner. It was all about making sure I could put it all together for the heats and then the finals.

After the session, Craig didn't hang about trying to find out what my fastest time was. 'How did he go?' I asked Dad.

'He pulled out a flyer second to last lap,' Dad said. 'He's got that new engine too. It'll be close, Archie.'

The times went up. Craig was on pole, by a fraction of a second. Such a small margin, but to look at the way he was strutting around you'd think he'd beaten me by an entire straight.

Kyla squeezed my hand and whispered, 'Beat him good, Archie.'

'Do my best,' I said.

Dad nodded to Kyla, then said, 'Just make sure you both keep away from young Silver. She's driving like she's got a demon inside.' But Kyla was on ten and Silver back on seventeen. She wouldn't be bothering either of us.

On the grid, I shut both her and Craig out of my head, tuning my focus to the race ahead. My plan was to be patient, to watch, wait and seize my chance when it came — as it would.

Craig was just as determined to shut me out, to keep me in second. The starter let us go. Round we went in formation for the rolling laps, Craig setting the pace. We did two laps before the lights went out and we were racing.

He was driving well, nailing each corner, exiting

without losing a fraction of time. I sat in behind, alert and waiting; circuit after circuit, me slipstreaming along the straights and giving him the love-taps on the corners. He stuck to the lead, driving like a pro.

Three laps to go, he hadn't made a mistake and we were lapping the back markers. Craig picked off number 82. I followed as if my kart was glued to Craig's. Number 47 on the straight ahead. Silver's. I dropped back a fraction. Craig pulled out to pass. She held her line, but he went so wide his wheel caught the grass. I snuck through the gap between them.

Craig was there behind me at the next corner, thumping the back of my kart. Two laps left . . . Final lap. Time to go for broke, to give it everything. But he was still there, hunting me down, doing his best to make me lose my nerve.

The finish line ahead, and I was over, beating him by vital fractions of a second.

Thanks, Silver.

Kyla came in seventh. Her parents had huge smiles on their faces as they came to meet her. Dad gave me the shoulder squeeze. 'Well done, Archie.'

Craig wasn't so pleased. He caught up with us as we walked back to base. 'That bitch should be banned. I'd have won if she hadn't blocked me.'

Kyla's dad said, 'Blocked you? Looked to me that you went wide.' To me he said, 'Nice piece of driving, Archie.'

Craig gave a hiss like a deflating tyre and took himself off.

Dad handed me his phone. The text from Grandad said: *V g*

Kyla and I watched the last races of the day, then we

locked everything up and went back to the motel.

Over dinner the talk was all racing. 'What happened to Silver?' I asked.

Kyla's dad said, 'There seemed to be something wrong with her engine.'

'That girl needs to race,' Dad said. 'Her father's worried sick about her. You two, just make sure you keep out of her way.'

'Should be easy enough,' I said through a huge yawn. 'Don't know about you lot, but it's an early night for me. Tomorrow's going to be a big day.'

THE MORNING WAS fine with a light wind and some cloud cover. Perfect — not too hot and not too cold. We hit the track when it opened and got busy checking and re-checking everything. Silver and her dad had her kart outside their tent working on the engine. Dad finished with my kart and went over to help out.

I collected Kyla and we joined a bunch of others to watch the first race. Craig, of course, had noticed the problem with Silver's kart.

'Serves her right. No engine can stand the sort of mauling she hands out.'

Nobody bothered answering him.

When our race was called, I asked Dad, 'Silver's kart okay?'

He shook his head. 'It's a bit dodgy still. We couldn't find the problem. It's one of those intermittent things — always difficult to work out exactly what's wrong. If you have to lap her again, just be careful.'

We took the kart down to the grid. Craig was there already and on pole thanks to being faster than me in qualifying. *Well, mate — a race is different from a qualifier.*

But I had work to do, and thinking about Craig wasn't it. I put on my helmet and focused on the race ahead.

The starter let us go for the rolling laps. The lights went out and I put my foot down, chasing Craig into the corner. We battled our way through eight laps, with me hustling him into the corners, letting him know I was there, letting him know I was waiting and watching.

Lap nine and a kart in front of us — 47. Silver. She was still ahead of us as we hit the back straight. Could have been that Craig lost concentration at the sight of her, but he went wide on the bend and left the door open enough for me to sneak through.

I caught Silver — aimed to pass her on the corner before the hairpin. Craig was right behind me, but I held back as Silver slowed. I'd seen her pull that trick before. She'd wait till the overtaking kart was level with her, then swerve out just enough to edge them off course. I waited till we'd driven past the apex and were heading for the exit, where I passed her before she could accelerate. I was almost up to full speed when I felt an almighty whack on the rear of the kart. I just had time to see Craig slip through before I was thrust out into the path of another kart. The world turned, and turned again. I was on the grass with a stalled engine.

Shit. What the hell was that?

Silver. Of course. She was off the track too, and I hoped she'd bloody stay off. Rage fired through me, but years of Dad's training kicked in. I started the engine again, and right away knew the set-up was stuffed.

A bent chassis was my guess. Bugger it, I'd drive the bloody race anyway.

I came last. The only halfway good thing was that Craig came in third, Ollie first and Lewis second.

Dad looked grim. 'Go to lunch, Archie. I'll see what I can do. Read this.' He shoved Grandad's text under my nose.

Next race 1st of day.

'Which I think means you have to drive the next race like nothing's gone wrong,' Dad said. He gripped my shoulder and gave it a squeeze. 'Hold it together, mate.'

'Yeah. I will. I am. Thanks, Dad.' But goddamn it. I was furious. To be bumped off the track like that — that was shit.

Kyla came to get me. 'You okay, Archie?'

I took her hand. 'Getting there. What happened?'

'Dad said she just turned right into the back of your kart and she didn't seem to be able to steer it when she hit the grass either. She didn't get back on the track anyway.'

I took a deep breath and stretched out my shoulders. 'Let's hope she's out for the rest of the day. Come on, I'm starving.'

We lined up at the canteen with others from our class. 'Hard luck, Archie,' Lewis said.

'You didn't pass me!' Jack sounded like he couldn't believe it.

'I will, old man. Don't worry your little head about that.'

'Where's Craig?' Tama asked.

'Daddy's probably got a chef in their trailer,' Sel said. 'It's the bacon and egg pie for me.'

Kyla and I ordered the lasagne, which came with a

rather limp salad. Nothing wrong with the garlic bread though.

As soon as we'd finished, I said good luck to the others and got up to leave. I was keen to shoot back to see how Dad was getting on, but Craig was coming in as I was going out. 'Hey, buddy, I need you,' he said.

'Later.'

He could wait. I wanted to find out about my kart.

CHAPTER SIXTEEN

DAD LOOKED UP. His expression wasn't encouraging. 'I've done the best I can with it. We'll have to get it fixed properly when we get home.'

Shit. More dollars washing down the drain. 'I'm going to drive it anyway.'

'Thought you would. It could have a bit of understeer coming into the corners. It'll be like driving a donkey where he doesn't want to go.'

'Anything I can do?'

'Yes. Grab me something to eat.'

'Sorry. Should have thought of that. Bacon and egg pie okay with you?'

Back in the clubrooms, Craig looked to be in the middle of making a speech. He saw me and beckoned. Stuff him, he wasn't my boss. I bought Dad his pie, then ambled over.

'What's up?'

'If you'd stayed around, you'd know and I wouldn't have to explain all over again.'

'What's biting you?' I asked. 'Your kart didn't get bent out of shape.'

He shoved the piece of paper he was holding under my nose. 'It's about getting our karts bashed up. I'm going to do something about it. Read this.'

It was a handwritten letter to the stewards. I read it aloud: *We, the undersigned, want Silver Adams banned from kart racing. The reasons are: she endangers other drivers; she causes crashes; she drives with the express intention of blocking karts behind her.*

There was a list of names printed underneath, mine included. Sel, Jack, Ollie, Tama and Kyla had all signed beside their names.

I dropped the paper on the table. 'I'm not signing that.'

The boys shuffled their feet, but Kyla's face relaxed as if she was relieved. Craig wasn't pleased. 'Archie the nice guy.' He thumped his fist down. 'Get off the fence, you wimp. Man up, for once in your life. Sometimes you have to make a stand.'

I picked up the letter. 'Watch me. I'm making a stand.' I ripped the paper in half, then in half again. 'It's a shit letter and a shit idea.' I stalked out, so furious I was shaking.

Kyla followed me with Dad's lunch. 'Here. You forgot this.'

I took it from her. 'You signed.'

'Yeah. As soon as I'd done it, I wished I hadn't. He's so persuasive, you know?'

'Bloody Jack put his name to it too. And look at how many crashes he causes.' There was a handy can on the ground — I booted it.

'He doesn't do it on purpose. But Silver does.'

I sighed, and took hold of Kyla's hand. 'Yeah. I've got the kart to prove it.'

'**YOU TOOK YOUR** time,' Dad said.

Kyla gave him a run-down of the drama.

'It's a taste of what happens when you get up into the big leagues, Archie. Get used to it. Now buzz off and let me concentrate here.'

We went outside. I didn't have much hope that Dad would be able to get my kart competitive before the next race. Disappointment bit deep.

'What are you going to do?' Kyla asked.

'If it can move forwards, I'll drive it.'

She smiled and gave my hand a squeeze. 'Archie — why didn't you sign? You were pretty wound up.'

'He's bloody lucky I didn't rip *him* in half.'

She let a moment of silence go by before she said, 'So? Why didn't you sign? Craig was certain you would. He said, *Archie'll be furious. He'll sign.* I think that's what convinced the others.'

I didn't say anything for ages, but she didn't say anything either. In the end, I just came out with it. 'She lost her mother. I know what that's like.'

There wasn't much else to say after that. We headed back to the clubrooms. Craig wasn't there and things had calmed down. None of the guys said I was right to have torn up the letter, but they were just that extra touch friendly, making sure they came with me to look at the grid positions for the pre-final.

'Fourteen. Could be worse.' And, fate being the joker it was, Silver was beside me on thirteen.

As we took the kart to the grid, Dad said, 'It's driveable, Archie. More than that I can't promise.'

'It's sweet, Dad. I'll go hard out. I'll try and make the top ten.'

'That's the spirit. Grandad sends his love.' He showed

me the love-sending text: *Drive it like you stole it. Beat every other bastard out there.*

'That's a long one. I bet he got Gran to type it.'

I pushed my kart into position. Silver turned her head to look at me for a full two seconds before she pulled on her helmet. I put my own helmet on. What the heck was up with her? That look was pure poison.

I settled into my prep. The first thing to work out was how to get past her at the start.

'Start your engines.'

The starter counted us down and out of the dummy grid. I used the rolling lap to test the kart. It felt a million times better than before, but it wasn't right. Round we went, with me testing the steering and the handling as much as I could on each corner. It felt like the two shortest rolling laps ever.

The second we got the signal to race, I swerved across in front of Silver to take the inside. *A basher can't compete with experience, my friend.*

The first corner showed me how far out of true the kart was now. I did my best to compensate, but every corner I was losing time. The kart went in too deep, and by the end of the sixth lap there were nine drivers still in front of me. Silver wasn't one of them.

I passed number 35 coming out of the bend before the front straight. Didn't know who it was. Somebody up ahead went off on to the grass. I got through before he sorted himself out. I was eighth. I drove with fierce concentration, determined to hang on to that position. *Consistent. Be consistent.* I didn't worry about planning how to pass those in front of me. They'd all get past me again even if I did manage to sneak through.

I was aware of karts chasing me. I held on, corner

after corner, straight after straight.

Then — drama at the pointy end of the race. A kart spun out. It was Tama. Josh was behind him and followed him into the spin. Both of them ended up on the grass and I drove into sixth place.

Two more laps. *Keep it consistent. Don't try to be clever.*

The final lap board. *Keep it together. Forget about the pain in your shoulders, the cramp in your hands. Drive.*

The final straight and the start/finish line, with the official waving the chequered flag. The race was over. Sixth. Not bad. I'd got lucky, I knew that. Sometimes it happened. It helped balance out the bad stuff.

Dad met me with a grin on his face. 'Good driving, Archie. Bloody good driving. How's the kart?'

'Pig awful.' I flexed a few muscles and began stretching out my hands. 'Thanks, Dad. You're a bloody marvel.'

'We'll see if we can tweak it again. What's it doing?'

'Understeering into the corners. There's not much grip at the front on the exits either.'

'Right. That gives me something to work with.'

He wouldn't be able to get it perfect, but I'd do what I could with it in the final. 'Did Craig win?'

'Yep. Sel second, Ollie third, Lewis fourth. That Auckland guy, Hugh, he was fifth.'

Kyla was eighth and stoked. Silver came in at twenty-one.

That meant Craig would be on pole for the final. I hoped Dad had got my kart good enough to give him a fright, even if I couldn't beat him.

SEL PUSHED HIS kart on to two, looking mighty stoked. I caught his eye and gave him a thumbs-up. It was his best result ever.

I positioned my kart, then worked on shutting out the world. Focus, concentration, determination. This race and the present moment — that's all there was in the world.

The starter counted us down, out on to the track. Again, I used the rolling lap to test the kart as much as I could. It was better, but unless you get very lucky, you can't beat good drivers when the kart isn't set up one hundred per cent. All I could do was give it a bloody good try.

The lights went out, the power kicked in as we accelerated. The handling was better. Still unsteady at the back, but the understeer wasn't as bad.

Craig was leading, but Sel, Ollie and Lewis were hard on his tail, with the Auckland guy closing in on them. I concentrated on my own race.

I planned to pass Auckland guy half a straight ahead on the left-hander. All good. I slipped through, only to have him pass me again as we came out of the corner. The kart was just a fraction unstable on the exit, just enough to let him through.

If sixth was the best I could do, then I'd make sure he worked for his fifth place. Each corner we took, I hustled him, letting him know I was there, that I wasn't giving up. I passed him every opportunity I got, and each time he got through again on the exit. I didn't give in and I didn't give up.

Lap nine, he made the classic mistake. He looked behind. In that moment, I dived through and he didn't have enough time to get his focus back and catch me.

Fifth, and half a kart length between me and Lewis. I caught him, but lacked the power to get through. I followed him round the final bend, slipstreaming along the straight to the chequered flag.

Fifth. Not what I'd aimed for, but I was proud of it. Craig, of course, had won with Ollie second, Sel third, Lewis fourth, and then me.

Dad was happy. 'Good work, Archie. Bloody good work.'

The text from Grandad was: *Yr bloody marvels. The pair of you.*

We laughed. Gran was definitely doing the typing.

We left our karts in the impound area for checking. Craig, all smiles and good humour now, said, 'Good job, Archie. Considering.'

Beside me, Kyla gave a snort of laughter. I laughed too — you had to, with Craig doing his *great man* act. It was either laugh at him, thump him, or spew.

We had to listen to his winner's speech too. I didn't mind applauding him, though. I'd done okay. We'd get the kart fixed. Craig wouldn't be so pleased with himself at the end of the next Challenge meeting.

Silver didn't go to the prize-giving dinner. She'd disappeared right after the final race. That was probably the best decision she'd made all day.

CHAPTER SEVENTEEN

BACK HOME, ERICA greeted Dad like he'd been stuck in Antarctica for a year. I left them to it and got to work washing my gear.

I was shoving my racing suit into the washing machine when Felix appeared beside me.

'Hiya, Buster. Did you get plenty of Easter eggs?'

He ignored that. 'Tell me about the races.'

Tricky. I had a think while I set the machine going. 'Your mum won't like it, mate.'

'I'll help. I'll clean it.' He gestured in the direction of the garage.

He sure was a determined little rat. 'Let's do it then. It'll give them time to get the kissing done with.'

He shuddered. 'Yuck.'

Off we went to sort out the trailer, and clean and check the kart. I described each race, figuring that he'd soon get bored of it. But no. His eyes got bigger and shinier, and I reckoned we'd be having a few interesting discussions with Erica quite soon.

The discussion with her came sooner than I expected. The second event in the Challenge series was at Tokoroa the next weekend, so there was a fair amount of kart talk between me and Dad. Felix was away at his carer's during the day because of school holidays, but we did the kart talk in the evenings anyway when Dad got back from work. Felix kept his mouth shut and kept his head down as always. Erica didn't join in either, except that her face said a hell of a lot.

Tuesday we got the kart fixed. Wednesday we took it out to the track for a practice. I drove a few laps, came in so we could adjust one thing, then out for another few laps, and back in to tweak the next thing. It was dark by the time we drove home.

'Okay?' Dad asked.

'Yep. We're ready. The kart feels good again.'

Erica had dinner waiting for us. Man, her food was good. Plenty of it too. I tucked in. This was worth getting hungry for.

We'd just finished having seconds when old Felix announced, 'I want to go, too.'

'Go where, darling?' Big smiles that her little boy had actually said something.

'Tomorrow. I want to go.'

Erica's smiles vanished in a puff of exhaust smoke. 'Oh Felix, darling, I'm going to have to say no. It's just not safe. We'll do something nice tomorrow instead. I promise.'

He didn't say anything else, but I was getting to know that stubborn look on his face and it told me he hadn't given up.

The next afternoon as we were packing up to leave, I said to Dad, 'We'd better check for stowaways.'

'He wouldn't,' Dad said.

'He bloody would.' We checked, but unless he'd tucked himself under the wheel arches, he hadn't climbed on board.

As things turned out, I was pleased not to have him around. The day went brilliantly, for most of it. Grandad and Gran were there, with the promised feast for lunch. I drove some of the best races of my life, and I was the driver pushing his kart on to pole for the pre-final and the final. Craig was right there on second both times, and majorly pissed off.

It was the weather that stuffed things up. With four laps to go in the final, the rain came down. I pushed as hard as I could, going all out despite the lack of grip. Lost it on the second to last lap, when I spun going through the double left. I went off on to the grass. Got back on with no damage done, but I'd lost the lead with three karts ahead of me now. I couldn't see who they were for the spray kicking up off the track and the rain belting down.

There wasn't enough time to get past any of them. Fourth.

I thought about what that meant as I drove the cool-down lap. It meant that I'd have to win the next in the series to get the rest of the promised tyres. It also meant that Craig would be leading the Challenge with a second and a first. It wasn't a complete disaster, though. Only five of the six rounds counted. Today could be the one I dropped.

Craig greeted me with a fat smile. 'Those tyres will be mine. The sponsors like winners.'

Tama watched him stroll away. 'That's what I like about old Craig — he's such a humble winner.'

Grandad stomped around, cussing. 'Bloody weather. Get in some wet-weather practice before next time.'

'On slicks?'

'No, Archie. On snowshoes,' Dad said. 'Put it behind

you. Grandad's right. Some practice in the wet could be a good idea.'

Yeah. It was humiliating that Craig had driven so well. I didn't want to hand him another first by wandering off on to the grass.

WE GOT HOME late Sunday night, took the kart out of the trailer, then collapsed into bed. The morning arrived far too quickly — the night must have been turbo-charged. Then I remembered. Holidays. I shut my eyes and went back to sleep.

But not for long. Dad stuck his head around the door, a weird look on his face. 'Archie, can you get your butt out here for a tick?'

'It's holidays, Dad.'

'Please, son.'

Shit. I rolled out of bed.

'Boxers could be a good idea,' Dad said.

Well, it served him right if he didn't like the view — he was the one who'd dragged me out of bed when I was still asleep. I took my own sweet time about putting on trackies and a hoodie before I hit the kitchen.

I got the story after one look. Felix was sitting on a chair and holding tight to the kitchen table. Erica stood in the doorway, and it was too close to call as to who looked the most stubborn.

Dad cleared his throat — more to stop himself from laughing, I guessed. 'This is the situation, Archie. Felix is refusing to go to day care.'

'I want to help.'

'No, Felix. That's out of the question. Now will you get off that chair? You're making me late.' Erica wasn't doing too bad a job of keeping her temper, I'd give her that.

I gave a huge yawn. 'I'm not going anywhere today. Okay with me if he stays here.'

I thought about going back to bed, but I loved a good battle, and this looked like being a beauty. My money was on Felix. Just to even the odds a bit, I said to him, 'It won't be very exciting for you, buddy. I've got to write the report for my sponsors.'

'I'll be good.'

Shit. It was enough to make you cry. I didn't know what to say, so I took a look at Erica. She was at the pissed-off stage now, and impatient. She gave in.

'All right. But just this once, Felix. We are *not* going to have this performance ever again. Do you hear me?'

He kept his head down and his mouth shut. Quite an effective technique.

Erica and Dad left together, him with his arm around her. He said something to her and she rested her head on his shoulder for a second, then looked up at him and smiled.

My dad, the hero.

Meanwhile, I was the babysitter. 'You had breakfast?'

'Toast with jam.'

'I need eggs and bacon. You ever scrambled an egg?'

He hadn't. I gave him eggs to crack. He was pretty good at fishing the shell out of the bowl.

'Want some?' I asked when it was cooked. I put a spoonful on a plate for him without waiting for a reply. With Felix, you could be waiting all day for an answer. I put bacon on the plate too. If he didn't eat it, I would.

He ate the lot. What a guts.

We spent the morning working. He helped clean the kart, then when I started checking it I gave him the job of handing me the tools as I explained what I was doing. Finally, we tidied the trailer and washed my gear. As we worked, I gave him a corner-by-corner commentary on each of the races, and his eyes shone like polished axles. When I got to the final and told him the sad story of the rain and the grass, he looked ready to bawl.

'Listen, buddy. You've got to harden up. You can't let disappointment get hold of you. What you have to do is drive the next race and forget about the bad one.'

I'd heard those words of wisdom myself.

In the afternoon I set him up with his mum's iPad and showed him how to find karting videos on YouTube while I wrote my report. Then I skyped Kyla for an hour.

Late afternoon I was feeling a bit guilty about leaving him alone for so long, but he was fine, still watching karts race and spin and flip out. I hoped Erica wouldn't check the history.

'Come and help me cook,' I said.

We were still in the kitchen when the parents came home.

'How was your day?' Erica asked me.

'Fine. No problems.' I didn't give her time to say *Thanks but I'll make sure it doesn't happen again*. I turned to Dad. 'About that practice in the wet. We'll need some rain between now and Hamilton.'

'Won't be a problem, Archie. It's April. It's school holidays. Of course it'll rain. Every blasted day probably.' He looked at Erica and changed the subject so that for the rest of the meal we chatted about all of us going to a movie together. One big, happy family.

CHAPTER EIGHTEEN

THE THREE WEEKS between Tokoroa and the next in the series at Hamilton sped by. The last Thursday of the holidays it rained hard enough to float a boat. Dad figured we couldn't get a better practice day.

On the way out to the track, I said, 'It's a shame Felix couldn't come.'

By way of a reply, Dad said, 'Erica had to stitch a car accident victim back together just yesterday.'

We turned off the main road and picked our way through the potholes to the track. 'Wet enough for you?' Dad asked.

'I'll be needing fins if it gets any worse.' But I intended to get out there despite the weather. I'd been thinking about that race at Tokoroa and I was determined I wouldn't ever get caught again by lack of technique on a wet track.

Dad helped me get the kart on to the grid, then he scuttled back to find some shelter. Couldn't blame him.

I got very, very wet. I had to do more laps than usual to warm up the engine. Then it was time to go hard out. I drove twenty laps all up. Went off eleven times. Did a couple of 360s. Felt like I was losing it on every corner. It was cold. My hands went numb, feet not far behind. But I drove the final six laps smoothly. I kept the kart on the black stuff and more or less held the line through the corners.

I was relieved when Dad waved me in. Hypothermia felt like it was waiting to pounce. He had to help me out of the kart I was shivering so much.

'Worth it, was it?' he asked.

'Shit, yeah.' I stood in the trailer to dry off and change my clothes. Still cold.

'You know how aggressive you can be in the wet now?'

I had to laugh. 'Sure as heck know how aggressive I can't be.'

FELIX CAME HOME and made a bee-line for the garage while I was doing the routine checks on the kart. I let him help with cleaning some tools, and taught him how to spin the wheel bearings. 'If they sound noisy, we replace them.'

'Did you do good today?' he asked.

So I gave him the story of each lap, of how I'd tried various ways of driving with the lack of traction until I was more confident. He looked as if I was feeding him burgers and fries.

At dinner, we didn't mention the practice. All was happy families again until Dad said, 'Thanks for helping with the kart, Felix. You did a great job out there.'

Felix seemed to light up from the inside. Erica had her usual struggle with her face. But what did she expect? That we wouldn't mention driving anywhere her little boy could hear? *Get real, lady.*

Life went on. The holidays ended.

Craig tried a spot of psychological warfare. First it was a text. *Looking forward 2 yr last race on free tyres?*

I thought about that for an hour or two, trying to dream up a smart comeback. I couldn't so I ignored it. I was busy — and he ought to be as well. School was manic. Grass kept growing.

Craig texted every few days. I didn't reply and I didn't waste any energy on thinking about his dumb messages or about him. I did manage to skype Kyla every few days. Sometimes we just did our schoolwork together. The good side of that was we got it done. The downside was that I could look but I couldn't touch. Still, my Skype sessions with her were islands of calm — until she told me about the prize money on offer in Hamilton.

'A thousand bucks for first place? You're kidding me!' But I was busy bringing up the website as I spoke. 'Hey, you're not kidding!' I started laughing. 'What's the betting Craig goes mental over this?'

He was keeping it to himself if he was. His text that evening was: *Control calling Archie. Come in pls. U worried, mate?*

Bugger him. *Yep. Worried. Frantic. Yah de yah. Thnx 4 caring.*

Interesting that he didn't mention the prize money. He'd know about it, though — he always knew stuff like that.

He sent another dumb text in the morning. Yes, this was a definite campaign. But it was having the opposite effect to what he was aiming for. It made me more focused than ever. Every spare moment I could get, I read karting info on the net or in magazines. I also viewed as many videos as I could to analyse driving techniques. If Felix happened to park his butt alongside me and listen as I explained what a driver was doing, then that was his affair.

Erica, though, was no fool. She knew what was happening and she took her own sneaky steps to put a stop to it. At dinner, would you believe, she started in on telling us about her day in Casualty. 'So sad,' she said, 'this young boy. Only fifteen and he's wrecked for life.' She knew bloody well that I was fifteen.

Dad shot me a look, but said nothing. No way was I going to ask what happened. Felix didn't lift his eyes from his plate.

But Erica didn't need encouragement. She launched into a detailed description of blood, shattered bone and escaping brain tissue. She told us what part of the boy's brain it was from and the effect that would have on his life.

You bitch. Play fair, or get off the track. I put down my knife and fork, then I eyeballed her. 'If you pull this stunt again then I'm going to do everything I can to encourage the kid to race. I'll find him a—'

'That's enough,' Dad said. He gave me a look I interpreted as *Keep it cool, mate*, and he gave his girlfriend a look that I couldn't interpret.

Silence. Erica's face went red but her mouth was clamped shut. I finished my meal. Felix left half of his. Jeez, that poor kid. Control freak for a mother.

'Finish that up, mate,' I said. 'You're helping me with the dishes.'

You'd think I'd given him a present. He even flicked me one of his nano-second smiles. But old Erica, she let out a moan and dropped her head in her hands. Felix's face crumpled. I put my hand on his shoulder so he'd look at me, then I rolled my eyes.

We shut the door between the kitchen and dining room. Those two needed to have a serious talk and I didn't want to hear a word of it. She might tell Dad she was packing up and leaving. I hoped she would. No, I didn't. Dad still behaved like she was better than a hot meal on a cold day. I'd even miss Felix. Shit. What a mess.

My phone went. It was another text from Craig. I read it out to Felix: '*Getting 2 Ham midday Thurs. U?* He's trying to make me worried.'

'Because you can't get there till the night?'

'You're dead right, my man. Want to give me a hand with the inventory?'

Stupid question. His eyes lit up and he was out the door a good half second before I got myself off the grid.

I ended up putting the rat to bed that night. There was no sign of his mother or my father. I guessed they were holed up in the bedroom. She'd be ranting at Dad, or crying. He'd be calm but his voice would get that edge to it. It was never nice to be on the receiving end of a bollocking when Dad's voice got edgy.

Or she could be packing and he could be crying.

Oh, the joys of life in the fast lane.

I didn't read Felix a bedtime story. Instead, using a diagram of the Hamilton track, I talked him through my race tactics.

Dad hadn't shown up by the time I went to bed. Neither had Erica. I wouldn't let myself think about what might be happening in that bedroom. It could be good, or it could be bad. Either way, I made damn sure I didn't hear a squeak of it.

The morning came and rolled out the same as always. Erica was brisk and trying to hurry Felix up. He ate at his usual slow pace. I used my mouth only to eat. Dad didn't look upset, so what the hell it all meant, I had no clue. Off the three of them went in a happy family bunch together. I got on my bike and rode to school.

I got a text from Dad just before classes started. He must have sent it as soon as he got to work: *Progress.*

They'd probably had make-up sex. Niiiiice.

Then I got another text. Craig again, but I was glad to be distracted from thoughts of Dad and Erica.

At lunchtime, Craig texted again: *Track in Hammy in top condition. C u 2morrow.*

'What's wrong?' Ginnie asked.

'Nothing.' I read out the text. 'It's from Craig. What he's really saying is *Ha ha I'm here already, nice and rested, but you've got a long drive in front of you. You'll be tired and I'm gonna beat the shit out of you.*' I told them about his psychological campaign and about the thousand dollars of prize money. 'There's the tyres too. If I don't win at Hammy, he gets those as well.'

'We'll hex him for you again,' Nina said.

'We'll have to do it by remote control,' Silas said. 'Hamilton's a bit far away.'

'My hexes work best at a distance,' Nina said.

Colin's hand landed on my back. 'Go hard, mate. We'll be back here cheering for you.'

He wouldn't be. He'd be up to his ears in mud on a rugby field.

'How's the kid?' James asked. 'You turned him into a speed freak yet?'

'No chance of that happening any time soon. Erica's

got a thing against racing. Says she'll move out rather than let her baby race.'

The five of them stared at me. 'Does she mean it?' James asked.

'Yeah. She means it.' I gave them a run-down on the dinner discussion about the escaping brain tissue and how she and Dad had done the vanishing act till breakfast this morning.

'She didn't say anything during breakfast?' Nina asked. 'No threats? Nothing?'

'Nope. Business as usual.'

'Ha!' said Ginnie. 'Betcha they had make-up sex.'

'D'you mind! I'm trying not to think about it. I don't know what happened.'

Colin thumped my back. 'Get real, Archie. She didn't walk out. She didn't give you the evils the second she sighted you today. It's a done deal. They did the rumpy pumpy.'

I was glad when the bell went. I'd rather drive ninety laps on slicks on a wet track than discuss my father's sex life.

The day was punctuated by three more texts from Craig. I didn't read them. I got away as quickly as I could after school. Dad would have the van and the trailer ready. All I'd have to do was park my bike and jump on board.

But it didn't happen quite like that. The first thing I saw was Erica, then Felix — but hang on a minute . . . that kid was bouncing off the walls. I caught sight of Dad, who just winked at me. Felix barrelled right at me and flung his arms around my middle.

'I'm coming too! I'm going to watch you race.'

I patted his back. 'We'd better get going then.'

I looked at Erica, a huge fat question in my face.

She looked right back. 'You'll look after him, Archie. I know you will. And thank you for putting him to bed last night.'

Women! No chance of guessing how they were going to react.

'Time we were on the road,' Dad said.

Off we drove, leaving Erica waving till we turned the corner.

'Okay then?' I asked.

'Yep,' said my father, looking very pleased with himself. 'All good. And we've got ourselves a helper.'

Felix might hate the whole weekend. It was noisy and the days were long. We wouldn't be able to take much notice of him — me especially. I had races to win, tyres to secure and prize money to chase. But every time I turned to see how he was getting on, I got the hugest beaming grin. He was enjoying himself so far anyway.

CHAPTER NINETEEN

I WAS BUSTING to ask Dad what had happened. I wanted to find out exactly how he'd made Erica change her mind. Surely Felix would fall asleep sooner or later so that I could extract the info from Dad? But the kid was amped and on high revs. It was like somebody'd taken the lid off and let him loose. There was just about a running commentary coming from the back seat. 'Craig's kart is 19 and he's our biggest rival.'

Our.

'That's right,' Dad said. 'What d'you reckon our chances are, Felix?'

I waited for a quick, and positive, answer — but he thought about it for so long that I turned around to check he was still there. He was looking worried.

'Spit it out, Felix. What's bugging you?'

'What if it rains? Craig might have practised in the wet too. He might win again.'

I let Dad field that one. 'That's racing, Felix. Sometimes you get it right, and sometimes you don't. You've just got to get back on board next time and drive like hell.'

And so the kilometres ticked away. We stopped for dinner at Taihape and the kid finally nodded off just before Taupo.

'He's out to it,' I said, 'so tell me. How come?'

My father doesn't do smug all that frequently, but when he does, he makes a good job of it. He drove for about a kilometre, just keeping quiet and looking damn pleased with himself. Then he got serious. 'She was going to leave, Archie. She really was. She's so dead against all motor sport.'

'Come on, Dad! She must patch up injuries from rugby, snowboarding . . .'

'She's a woman, son. All she wants is for her boy to be safe.'

I snorted. 'Wrapping him up in cotton wool won't do it.'

'That's what I told her. Teach him to drive now, then stand back, keep your fingers crossed and hope like hell nothing goes wrong.'

'Is that what you do?' I'd never imagined he worried when I was racing.

'Yes and no,' he said. 'You're a good driver, Archie. And you've got a good head on your shoulders. We prepare one hundred per cent.' We drove round a couple of corners in silence, then he said, 'But your grandad and I — we've both been out there in the thick of it. We know the risks. We know what can happen.'

'You still want to be racing, don't you? The pair of you.'

He laughed. 'Dead right. But the reflexes aren't there any more. And I have to say, we get such a buzz out of seeing you drive a good race. I'm proud of you. So's Grandad, although he'd rather die than tell you that.'

Nice, but I still didn't get why Erica had done a complete u-turn. 'But why did . . .'

'Erica change her mind? We just talked about what

sort of people she wanted in her son's life. What sort of man she wanted him to grow up to be. I asked her how Felix would feel if she walked out.'

Possibly he'd learnt that last question from me, since neither he nor Mum had asked me what I thought about her leaving. 'Did she say he'd think it was his fault? And did she say he'd hate her?'

'She got there in the end.'

Time to stop where this conversation could be headed and to ask him something else I was curious about. 'Where's his father? Dead or disappeared?'

'Neither,' said Dad. 'Felix is a test-tube baby.'

'You're kidding me! For real?'

'Yep. When Erica turned thirty-eight and the relationship hadn't happened, she decided to have a baby and bring him up by herself.'

I thought about that for a good couple of ks. 'He'll never know who his father is, then?'

'Yes, he knows. She's given Felix a photo of him and he's met him a couple of times. He lives in the UK — worked with Erica when she was over there. They keep in touch at Christmas and he always sends Felix something for his birthday.'

Sheesh! This took some getting my head around. 'What about grandparents?'

'Erica's folks moved across the ditch to the Gold Coast a couple of years ago. She says they don't really approve of what she did. It makes her all the more protective of him. The decider for her about staying or going — she can see he's doing okay with us.'

Yes, and if I spelled it out it would go something like: *Your kid now manages to look people in the eye; your kid now actually speaks; your kid has found something that spins his wheels.* Thinking about it, I probably wouldn't use the spinning wheels bit — best not to rub her nose in it.

Felix didn't wake up when we got to the motel. Dad carried him in and we dumped him into bed fully clothed but without his shoes. It was late. We went to bed and set the alarm for six.

WE GOT TO the track as soon as it opened at 7.30 the next morning. We set up our base, with Felix shadowing us the whole way. Dad gave him jobs to do — it reminded me of when I was little. You get the crap jobs but it makes you feel important. Felix buzzed around putting air in the tyres, lubing the chain, and Dad got him to hold the fuel funnel for him. He didn't exactly have a grin on his face, but man — he looked happy.

I went out for my first practice run, came back in, and we adjusted the camber on the front stub axles to give more turn in. Then it was back on the track to check.

'They're not quite right,' I said when I came in.

'Could be the tyre pressure,' Dad said. 'Wish we knew what Craig's running his at.'

Craig, bugger him, was looking good, and he'd rather lose his front teeth than tell me his tyre pressures.

Dad tweaked the camber some more, but we left the tyre pressures for the moment. 'Only ever change one thing at a time, Felix,' he said. 'Otherwise you don't know what's made the difference.'

Felix nodded, eyes shining.

I went out for another run. The kart still wasn't running right.

We were back in the tent before either of us noticed that Felix was missing. Dad didn't seem bothered. 'He won't go far,' he said. 'He knows where he can and can't go.'

So, it hadn't taken him long to get bored after all. Erica would be delighted. 'We'll change the tyre pressures next, I reckon,' Dad said.

And right then Felix came running into the tent. '13.5 and 14.5.'

I didn't take any notice — I was still a bit pissed at him, to tell the truth. Dad though, smiled. 'That's not a bad guess, Felix.'

'It's true! It's real! And his best lap time is 38.84.'

He had my attention now. Every molecule of it. 'You're talking about Craig? Felix, old mate, he's pulling your leg. Drivers never tell the truth.'

He was just about hopping with frustration. 'It *is* true. He didn't tell me. I listened. He told Gary *Set-up's good. I'll leave the pressure at 13.5 and 14.5.* And Gary said *Lap time.* And Craig said *38.84* and he laughed and then he said *I'll be on pole.*'

It was our turn to laugh. I held up a hand. 'Put it there, Felix my man.'

His mother wouldn't recognise him — sparkling eyes, bouncing stride. Chatting. *Spying.* I laughed some more.

The tyre pressures turned out to suit my set-up too. I came back in, giving the thumbs-up to Dad and the junior mechanic a.k.a. spy.

'You'd better help me push the kart on to pole,' I said to Felix when we got close enough to Craig for him to hear.

Craig shook his head. 'You wish.' I don't think he noticed Felix.

We had more work to do on our set-up before I'd be able to beat his lap time, though. It was better but not perfect. 'It's stepping out on the turns. Just a touch, but enough to make a difference.'

We worked hard all morning. Dad adjusted the jetting, then the brakes. We experimented with my seat position but ended up with it in the original setting.

Midday we stopped for lunch. Felix vacuumed up a plateful of macaroni cheese. Dad got him to eat the salad too. 'Vegetables and protein, Felix. Got to have both to build a strong body.' He ate it without even screwing up his face. His mother would have a hard time believing it.

She phoned just as we were finishing. Dad had a chat that I did my best not to hear, then he handed over to Felix. 'She wants to talk to you, mate.'

'Mum! It's *awesome*!' He listened, nodded and gave Dad back the phone.

I'd have to explain to the kid one of these days that you can't actually hear a nod.

We got back to work. By the end of the day, I was happy with my set-up. I went all out on the final run and knocked a tenth of a second off Craig's best time.

That evening, Felix went to bed early. All the excitement had knocked him out. Dad stayed to do the babysitting duty and I went in search of company. Found it in the motel suite occupied by Sel and Ollie and their fathers. Jack and Tama were there, then Craig turned up, with Lewis and Josh not far behind.

It wasn't long before Craig started up about Silver again. 'They need to ban her, they really do. She's dangerous. You must've seen her.' He frowned at me. 'She blocked you twice that I saw.'

'No, she didn't. No worse than anyone else does. You included.'

'He's right, Craig,' Lewis said. 'She drove okay today. Not brilliantly, though. She's untidy so she's not quick. What's your problem?'

'She's a loose cannon. I still say she should be banned. I still say she's dangerous. You guys are going to be sorry you didn't support me.'

'Give it a rest, mate.' I changed the subject. 'Your old man coming down?'

'Yep. He's going to give the new car a run.'

I refused to play the game and ask what sort of car. So did the others, except for Josh who was too young to know better. 'What make?'

'Audi R8.'

'Well,' said Jack, 'my old man's coming too in his pride and joy. It's a Skoda.'

We laughed. But an Audi R8. That was some car. It was hard to get one up on Craig. It made me keener than ever to win.

CHAPTER TWENTY

IT WAS HOSING down when we left to return to our units. 'Let's hope it clears up by the morning,' Tama said.

'Either that, or it rains all day,' I said. 'None of this half-arsed, can't make up its mind stuff.'

In the morning it seemed I'd got my wish. The sky was grey but no rain was dripping out of it. Felix stared out the window, his whole body tense with worry.

'Archie, if it rains will you have to drive on slicks again?'

'We just have to wait till each race,' I said. 'We'll be on wets if it's hosing down.'

Dad put breakfast on the table. 'Get this inside you, Felix. We're going to need your help today.'

He didn't argue, although it was easy to see he was busting to get out to the track.

We got there in plenty of time, half an hour before the grandparents arrived. Grandad shook hands with Felix. Gran hugged him.

'How's the young bugger going?' Grandad asked Dad.

'It's okay, Felix,' I said. 'He means me. On the track.'

I left the four of them in the tent and went outside. I chose a spot by myself where I could see the track. I wasn't the only one standing alone, drawing my mind into a point of focus where all there was in the world was the track, the kart and the skill needed to drive to the max. I was confident we had the set-up as near-perfect as possible.

The loudspeaker clattered out a call for our tuning run. As usual, I chose a space halfway down the field. I wanted to use the run to get in some passing practice on this track. Silver was up the front, with Josh beside her. Craig wouldn't be happy about that.

I took the first three laps slowly, warming up the tyres and scuffing them in. Then I set to work picking off the karts ahead of me. Jack was no problem — but it's easy to get past a kart that's off on the grass.

I came up behind Craig and Silver after another lap but didn't close up on them immediately. Something weird was going on and I didn't want to get pulled in when it blew.

Round we went through the hairpin. Craig could have got past easily. What the hell was he playing at? He kept on following her into the corners even though she braked too early and accelerated too soon. Her kart just about leapt off the track, and still he stayed tucked in behind her.

He didn't pass her on the straight to the sweeper either. There had to be something wrong with his engine.

I decided to pass the pair of them on the long straight. I closed in as we came to the right-hander, then went wider than I normally would, just to be on the safe side. *Sweet.*

I left them behind and settled in to take the five still ahead of me. One after the other, I snuck past — had a tussle with Lewis before I made it, and Ollie wasn't too easy either. But I was one hungry mongrel. I wanted pole for the heats, and I wanted to keep it for the pre-final and the final. My time in the qualifying run would be the decider for the heats.

Dad, Grandad and Felix met me at the pits when I came in.

'All right?' Dad asked.

'Yep. All good.'

I got out. Dad and Grandad went to lift the kart on to the trolley, and Grandad said, 'Can you give me a hand here, Felix? I'm not as strong as I used to be.'

I grabbed Dad's camera and snapped a photo, just in case he wanted to show Erica her son's proud face.

'What was wrong with Craig's kart, d'you know?' I asked as we walked back to base.

Dad shrugged. 'All I know is he went storming off to the stewards.'

Just then, a guy in a steward's jacket tapped me on the shoulder. 'Archie Barrington? Can you come with me, please?'

I followed him to the tech shed. Craig was there, looking thunderous. His father was there, looking rich and powerful. Silver leaned against a wall, looking bored. Her father looked worn and worried.

The chief steward cut right to the chase. 'Archie, you were behind Craig and Silver for most of a lap. What was your impression of the way Silver was driving?'

I told it like it was. 'She braked early, then accelerated too quickly.' I glanced at Craig. 'What was wrong with your kart? I kept waiting for you to pass her.'

'She blocked me! She bloody blocked me all the way. She shouldn't be on the track. I keep saying it and nobody . . .'

The steward cut him off. 'Thank you, Craig.

You've had your say. Archie's statement matches our observations. Your protest is declined.'

Craig flung around and stormed off. His father shook hands with the stewards and followed. I stood with my mouth hanging open before I worked out I could go too.

'Sorry I dissed your driving,' I said as Silver, her dad and I left together.

She did her usual trick of not answering, but her dad said, 'Thanks, Archie. I don't know why Craig's got it in for her.'

I didn't know either, so I sent our spy to hang about to see if he could pick up any clues.

'Archie! That's not fair!' Gran said. 'They'll march him back here by his ear.'

Dad said, 'Calm down, Mum. They won't take a blind bit of notice of him.'

She worried until Felix ran back in, his face all concentration. 'The father said *Don't worry I'll find you another mechanic* and Craig said *Can't you make Gary stay* and the father said *You don't want a mechanic who doesn't want to be here.*'

Light bulbs came on all over the tent. 'Felix, you've done it again.' We did the high five and the handshakes, plus the hug from Gran.

He looked stoked, but said, 'I don't get it.'

'It's a bad thing to lose your mechanic. Especially in the middle of a series,' I said. 'He's getting mad at Silver because he can't yell at Gary.'

'I didn't think Gary'd last the distance,' Dad said. 'Young Craig needs a lesson or two about treating people right. It's my guess Gary got tired of being treated like the hired help.'

I wondered if Craig's father had come in his new car. I wouldn't ask. Craig would probably calm down if he could skite about something — and I was happy for him not to calm down, especially not before qualifying. But I was picking he would make sure he got a spot well away from Silver.

I was right. She put her kart up the front again, so Craig chose a spot well back. I put myself in the middle. They let us go and, as always in a qualifier, we spread ourselves out along the track. Clear space ahead, and go for broke — get the fastest time and don't worry about any other bugger.

I kept an eye on the data logger as the laps ticked by. Towards the end of the run I pulled out everything and just went for it. I'd done the absolute best I could. I'd be gutted if some other mongrel took pole off me after this.

When the grid positions went up for the heats, Lewis and Ollie beat me to the board. Lewis said, 'Archie, you fecker, you're on pole.'

He was on two, Sel was on three, Ollie on four and Craig was back on five.

'You can just about see the storm clouds over his head,' Sel said as we watched him stomp back to his tent.

'Poor lad,' Gran said when we got back to our base. 'You can't help feeling sorry for him.'

'Spoilt young pup. Needs to learn some manners,' said Grandad.

My heat was called. The four of us went down to the grid. Gran stayed behind the way she always did. She took her chair outside to sit with other spectators.

Dad and Grandad lifted the kart off the trolley. 'Our turn, Felix,' I said. 'Let's get number 24 on pole.'

Dad snapped another photo.

I pulled on my helmet and gloves, breathed out a sigh of satisfaction and slipped into my seat. There was the usual wait before we rolled off the dummy grid, and I knew every single driver would be doing the same thing. We'd all be closing out the world. We'd all be bringing our focus back to the race ahead of us. For those few minutes, that's all that would exist. Just each of us, our karts, the track and the other competitors. Awesome.

We got the signal and were off, round the track, keeping our positions until the lights went out.

It was a dream heat — one of those times when the driving isn't conscious. It just happened without me having to think about it. I was in front and I stayed in front. A couple of times Lewis appeared in my peripheral vision, but I held him off.

I drove the final lap aiming for consistency rather than going all out. I was ahead. I didn't need to take risks. There was no need to push the boundaries. There was no sign of Lewis as I crossed the finish line.

My support team was stoked. Felix helped Grandad lift the kart on to the trolley without being asked this time, and when we were safely back in our tent, he said, 'Craig drove a shit race, Archie.'

Dad let out a groan. 'Felix, your mum won't like you using language like that.'

The kid gave him a look of hundred per cent scorn. 'I won't say it round her.'

We cracked up, then Grandad said, 'The young fella's right, Archie. Craig did drive a shit race. Didn't get past anybody. Came in tenth.'

'Jack's going round like he's cock of the dung heap,' Dad said.

I stared. 'Jack passed Craig? For real?'

'Stayed on the track for the whole race,' Dad said. 'Got past Craig on the final lap.'

That would put a dent in Craig's ego.

The rain came down just before the start of the final race of the day. There was a mad scramble while everyone swapped their slicks for wets. Glad it wasn't me out there. Gran and Grandad didn't hang about to watch, but Dad, Felix and I did. There was enough carnage out there to give Felix major jitters.

WHEN I WOKE in the morning, it looked like the weather gods had got over their grump. The sky was grey and the rain had stopped.

It held off all morning. I nailed the second heat. Craig got his mind back on the job and beat Lewis and Ollie to take second, and that put him on six for the pre-final.

During lunch, I got a text from Colin. *Nina says is hex working?*

I texted back. *Yep. Need strong 1 this arvo tho.*

Done.

I laughed. The worrying thing was that if I did win today, then Nina would be convinced it was all down to her hexes. I turned the phone off. Didn't need the distraction.

We went back to our base under a dirty sky. 'Might rain,' Grandad said.

'No!' Felix shook his fist at the clouds. 'Don't rain!'

Nina's hex might have missed Craig and hit the weather instead. I was mighty thankful I'd done those laps in the rain at home.

CHAPTER TWENTY-ONE

THE TRACK WAS still dry when we lined up for the pre-final.

I slid into my seat, helmet on, world shut out. All I had to do was stay in front.

The starter let us go. Round we went. The lights went out — and we were racing.

I got a good start, holding Lewis off so that he couldn't duck across to take the inside. He was there, hunting me down each corner, each straight, with Ollie doing the same to him.

Spits of rain blurred on my visor.

Lap six and no sign of Lewis. Instead, it was Ollie nagging away at me. I held him off. Lap nine coming into the hairpin, Craig popped up beside me, crowding to force me to put the inside wheels off the track.

No you don't, you prick. I flicked the steering and fed him a wheel. It pushed him wide, leaving me room to hold my line.

He fought me every turn of the track. Each straight, he was up there where I could see him. We'd hit the corner and he was behind me again, bumping the back of my kart. No way was I going to let him through. He wouldn't expect me to. No, he'd be aiming to unsettle me, to force me into making a mistake.

This was what it'd be like in Europe. *Thanks, Craig. Good of you to give me the practice.*

He moved out beside me when we turned the corner to the finishing straight. I could see him, swaying backwards and forwards, trying to push more speed out of his kart.

We crossed the line. I was pretty sure I'd beaten him. I hoped like hell I had. He didn't deserve to win.

The faces of my support crew confirmed I'd won.

'Played rough, did he?' Dad said as we pushed the trolley back to base.

'Tried to force me off the track. Then bumped me the rest of the race.'

Grandad said, 'You could protest.'

'No. I beat him. I'm not wasting fifty bucks on him.' As well as the cost of protesting, there was the time. Craig would appeal and the whole thing would drag on.

Dad nodded. 'Good decision.'

'But he cheated!' Felix said, outraged. 'That's not fair!'

'You're right,' Grandad said. 'But sometimes it's best to roll with the punches. Archie stayed focused. That probably made Craig angry. Angry drivers make mistakes.'

Felix wasn't happy.

I wasn't happy about the weather. The sky was getting darker and the wind had gone from pesky to blustery. While we checked the kart before the final, Felix kept ducking out to look at the conditions. 'It's raining!' he shouted. 'It's bloody raining!'

I stuck my head out of the tent. 'It's only drizzling, mate. Not enough to wet the track.' I watched the race for a moment. 'See? It's not bothering anyone.'

'This could get interesting,' Dad said as my final was called and we headed down to the grid.

'You should change,' Felix said. 'Look! It's raining!'

I shook my head. 'Still not enough to wet the track. It would cut up the wets on a track this dry.'

I shut the Tokoroa final out of my mind and instead went over the knowledge I'd gained from the drenching practice session back home. My idea was to hang on to the lead. I wouldn't put any money on the rain holding off, and I wanted to be out of the spray zone if and when it did come.

The starter gave us an evil grin as he let us go. Round we went in formation, then we were away.

Spits of drizzle blurred my visor on the fourteenth lap. Cleared again half a lap on. The track stayed dry. I was leading, but Craig, Lewis and Ollie were all there, hunting me down.

The drizzle started up properly as I came up to the final lap sign. I crossed the start/finish line for the last lap, and the sky took that as a signal to let loose.

I am not going to lose this race.

I had the advantage of being out front. I took the turn at the top of the straight as if I had full grip. Took in a bit of grass. No problems, though. I didn't worry about hitting my braking points and I drove much wider lines through the corners than usual. But I got round and hadn't lost enough speed for those behind to catch me. But each corner was a dice with fate. Stay on the track, or slide off forever. Twice I went wide enough to hit the grass, but I kept two wheels on the black stuff. I used what I'd learned in the practice at home. The driving wasn't pretty, but it wasn't untidy enough to get me into trouble.

The final turn up to the finish. I put my foot down, wrestling with the wheel to drive a vaguely straight line. The rain was belting down so bloody hard now my peripheral vision was useless. I just drove hard out and hoped like hell.

I've never been so pleased to see the chequered flag. I crossed the line, eased back on the power, turned to look behind me to see where the others were — and went off the end of the straight. Idiot. But I didn't care. I'd won. In the rain. On slicks.

I got out, turned my kart around and, when the last of the drivers had passed, pushed the kart back on the track and drove quietly into the pits.

My crew were waiting for me. Gran was there too. She looked proud and she was smiling. Felix was like a bee in a bottle — all buzz and fizz. 'Archie! You won! You won the tyres and you won a *thousand* dollars!'

'Bloody good driving,' Grandad said, three times.

We left the kart to be checked for compliance.

Silver's dad came up to us. 'Excellent driving, Archie. Congratulations.'

'Thanks,' I said. 'How did Silver get on?'

'She did okay. Came in nineteenth.'

We watched him walk away and I got the feeling he didn't give a rat's about his daughter's results. All he seemed to care about was that she got on the track. But as far as I could tell, racing wasn't helping her deal with her mother's death. He must've thought it would. I wondered how long he'd keep driving her round the country.

'Craig came in right behind you,' Dad said. 'Half a second.'

'Shit! Glad I didn't know he was that close!'

We laughed. I'd won. It was beginning to sink in.

Craig and his father didn't hang about. Gary watched them leave in the Audi, disgust on his face.

'I hear you're leaving,' Dad said.

Gary spat on the ground. 'Arses. The pair of them. If I didn't have to get back to Auckland myself, I'd leave their bloody van and trailer here.'

We took him back to our tent where Gran had hot drinks waiting, along with a tin full of three types of homemade biscuits. I ate two of each and Felix wasn't far behind.

Time to pack up, then it was prize-giving. I was looking forward to that, running a few sentences of my speech through my brain.

Sel ducked into our tent out of the rain. 'Good race, Archie. Not that I could see you for all the spray. Hey, did you hear? Craig and his old man have gone already.'

'Bad sportsmanship,' said Grandad. 'They should have waited for prize-giving and Craig should have made a speech too.'

I didn't care. It was fine by me that he wasn't around to spoil my moment in the spotlight. 'How did you get on?' I asked Sel.

'Fifth. Bummer, really. I should've gone all out like you did.'

But he'd had the spray in his face and karts all around him. Much trickier to go all out under those circumstances.

I enjoyed every nano-second of prize-giving. They gave me a trophy, and the cheque for a thousand dollars. Then I launched into my thank you speech. Thanked everybody you usually thanked, including Gran for feeding us. 'But I'll have to go easy on the homemade biscuits or I'll be racing in the heavy class.' Laughter. Always good. I finished by saying, 'And lastly, big thanks to little bro Felix. Awesome job today, Felix. Thanks mate.'

He was quite chuffed.

I couldn't afford to get too pleased with myself, though. Craig was ahead on points thanks to his one win and two seconds in the Challenge so far. I had two wins, but that fourth place meant he was in a better position because I couldn't afford another bad result. He could come in last, drop that round and still beat me.

I did not want him, or anyone else, to do that.

CHAPTER TWENTY-TWO

IT WAS HARD work waking up the next morning. We'd got home late, or early depending on how you looked at it. Felix slept most of the way.

But the alarm went, and school was waiting. That trophy was looking damned good on my shelf.

By the time I got myself to the breakfast table, Felix was already in mid-flow, describing the day to his mum. Erica's face was doing that switch from thrilled to not so thrilled, but I have to say this for her — she asked him questions and she smiled in the right places.

Nice to see Felix so chatty, but I was quite glad to be left in peace after the two of them tootled off with Dad. I needed to get my head together for school.

There, as predicted, Nina's first words were, 'My hex worked! Aren't you glad I'm on your side, Archie?'

'Yep,' I said. 'You're one scary dame.'

But they were all rapt I'd won. Colin's rugby team had won as well. A good weekend.

'So you're beating that Craig guy? He's eating dust?' Silas asked.

I shook my head. 'It's all done on points. He's got 257 so far and I've got 256.'

'Nothing in it, then,' Colin said. 'Three more rounds. Plenty of time.'

'When's the next one?' Silas asked.

'End of July. Bay of Plenty.'

Three whole months away, with only a couple of club days between now and then.

Not that the time dragged. I kept in touch with Kyla and my other friends as much as I could. The news came that the European venue was Portugal. I read up about the track on the net. Read some stuff about the country as well. Portugal. My heart gave a kick. I *had* to win the Challenge.

School seemed to think mid-year exams were a nifty idea. Teachers kept on expecting assignments to be done. Life as usual, except that now Felix came with us to club days. His eyes still shone and he held his head up as he bustled around the club rooms, or stood on the sidelines to watch. Erica didn't talk about it, but one day soon her little boy was going to ask to race. Then the sump oil would hit the fan.

Towards the end of the term, Kyla skyped me with good news. 'Archie! I'm coming to Wellington for the first week of the holidays. You going to be around?' She was all lit up and bouncing in her seat.

I just sat there, grinning at her, then said, 'I'll make bloody sure of it. When do you get here? Where are you staying?' Thanks to Erica and Felix, we didn't have a spare room any more.

But she was staying with her auntie. The good thing about that was it wasn't too far from mine.

The day she was due to arrive turned out to be stormy — typical holiday weather. I hoped like hell it wouldn't mess up her flight, but when I got to the airport — half an hour early — the arrivals board said it was on time.

Outside, the wind blew and the rain fell, but her plane landed and there she was coming towards me, a wide bright smile lighting her face. I ran and threw my arms around her. She dropped her gear and we kissed.

'Ha!' said a voice behind us. 'I see that it wasn't for love of me you were so keen to spend a week at my house!'

Kyla let me go and gave a woman of about Gran's age a smacker of a kiss on the cheek. 'But you come a very close second, Joanna!'

The auntie rolled her eyes, then shook my hand. 'Pleased to meet you, Archie. Call me Joanna — unless you want to live dangerously.'

I grinned back at her. 'I'll save the danger for the track, thanks.'

It turned out she was a great-aunt and a kind of stand-in grandmother, and she'd just come back from doing something with slum kids in the Philippines. The two of them teased each other and swapped family gossip all the way back to Joanna's house. I worked on a plan to whip Kyla away so we could hang out for the rest of the day.

It didn't quite work like that. We had to have lunch with Joanna. Then we had to look at the photos of her trip. The thing was, she was doing it deliberately. Even though she kept a straight face, she couldn't keep the gleam out of her eyes.

Go with the flow, Archie. I kept quiet, hoping Kyla would slam the brakes on sooner rather than later.

After we'd done the photos *and* the souvenirs, Joanna said, 'Now I'm going to show you my teaspoon collection. You'll be fascinated, Archie. I've got . . .'

'Teaspoons!' Kyla yelped. '*You!* Yeah, right! And anyway, we're going to disappear now. Goodbye, auntie dearest.' She grabbed my arm and tugged me away. We ran out of the house with the sound of laughter chasing us.

'Is she always like that?' I asked.

'No,' said Kyla. 'She's usually worse. We got off lightly. I think she likes you.'

'I'll try not to make her change her mind then. What d'you want to do with the rest of the day?'

'Sit somewhere out of the weather and watch the sea. One day, I'm going to live by the sea and I'll build me a house where I can watch it all day.'

We caught the train into town, then a bus out to Lyall Bay where we got a window table at Maranui café right on the beach above the crashing waves.

We talked and talked, so that the afternoon flew by. And then I remembered — it was my night to cook. I needed to get going. 'Wanna have dinner at ours?' I asked.

She shook her head. 'Not worth the hassling I'd get from Joanna. Another night, though.'

The week sped past so quickly. Sometimes we went out to a movie, or else we had a cheap but reasonably healthy meal in town and just hung out. A couple of times we went to Silas's house with my mates and watched DVDs. Kyla — and Joanna — came to dinner on Thursday night, but I was pleased that Erica offered to be the chef.

Felix got grumpy with me on Friday. 'You keep going out with that girl. You should stay home.'

Dad said, 'It's called young love, Felix. You wait. Girls get a lot more interesting as you get older.'

Felix did the trick of dropping his head and keeping

his mouth shut. Erica looked worried. Dad laughed. 'It could be worse, mate. Now, how about you come and give me a hand with that lounge door. I reckon we're going to need to re-hang it to stop the bloody thing sticking.'

I escaped as Felix was squatting beside Dad, examining the hinges, and Erica was looking relieved.

'Would you believe it?' I said to Kyla when we met a couple of hours later. 'Felix is jealous of you.'

'Well, of course he is, thicko! He's had your undivided attention till now.'

I didn't like it. It felt weird — as if he had some claim on me.

'Look,' my girlfriend said, 'the kid worships the ground you walk on. You can't take him along for the ride, then toss him out when it suits you. That's not how families work. At least, they're not supposed to.'

I wondered if she'd remembered that my mother had pretty much done that to me. I sighed. It still niggled at me. Why had she? There had to be more to it than her and Dad just being too different.

Kyla slid her arm around my waist. 'You've gone all quiet.'

'Thinking does that to a bloke. D'you really think — do you reckon that Felix really . . . ?'

'Sees you as his big brother? There ain't no debate about that, my friend.'

We didn't talk about it any more, but it lurked in the back of my mind for the rest of the evening, bugger it. As we were heading to the station for her to catch the train back to Joanna's I said, 'If Erica wasn't so bloody paranoid about racing, we could take him out to the track over the weekend.'

'We could start with indoor go-karts,' she said. 'You could ask your mates along as well. And Bill and Erica.'

I laughed. Why hadn't I thought of that? Not even Erica could object to indoor driving. 'Joanna could come too.'

◉

FELIX WAS IN bed when I got home. I made the love birds a cup of tea and put the suggestion to them.

'Good thinking, Archie,' Dad said.

'No. Absolutely not,' Erica said.

I took my own cup of tea and went off to my room. Bloody Erica. If she wanted me to be a big brother to her son, then she should bloody well let me *be* one.

I sat at my desk, trying to calm down. Stupid to get my chassis twisted over this. She was just trying to keep her little boy safe.

But — I crashed a fist on to the desk. Spilled the tea. Didn't care. She couldn't have it both ways. Let him loose or keep him wrapped up. Not this half-arsed, neither one thing or the other racket.

Before I'd really worked out that it was time she learned a few things, I was on my feet and walking. I crashed open the door to the lounge. Didn't mean to, but Dad and Felix had stopped it sticking.

'I've got something to say.'

Dad raised his eyebrows but gave me a small nod. *Go for it.*

Erica looked like one of those plants that shuts itself up when it gets touched.

Too bad. I eyed her fair and square. 'Do you want me to be a big brother to Felix? I don't want the lecture. Just give me a yes or a no.'

She wasn't stupid. She snapped her mouth shut and sort of moaned like something was pulling her in half. Dad put both arms around her. 'He's got a point, darling. And you've known this was coming. You're going to have to decide. One way or the other.' He flicked his head in the direction of my room.

I was plenty glad to leave them to it. If she was gone by morning, her kid with her, it'd be fine by me.

Bloody hell. Who was I kidding? I'd miss the little ankle biter. Families. It looked like one had snuck up on me and I hadn't even glimpsed it in my peripheral vision.

CHAPTER TWENTY-THREE

IN THE MORNING when I hit the breakfast table, Erica was there and eating. Felix was giving me the silent treatment which, in his case, meant he didn't hand me one of his quick smiles, and Dad was imitating an expressionless statue. I helped myself to hashed spuds and eggs. They really should put the radio on. This silence was not cool.

I sat down and started eating.

Erica took in a couple of breaths — on her way to hyperventilating if she wasn't careful. I figured we were about to discover which way she'd crumbled the cookie.

Yep.

'Felix, Archie's got a surprise for you,' she said. Then, to me: 'It's all booked. We've got a slot for the whole place this afternoon if you want to ask your friends.' She looked sick, and for a split second I saw an image of the skull with the escaping brain tissue.

For the first time, I felt a bit sorry for her. 'Will you and Dad come too?'

'Where? What?' Felix looked at her, then at me, then at Dad.

She gave a sort of sob. 'No. I can't.'

Dad stood up so he could hold her shoulders. 'Yes,

you can. And yes, we will. Archie, that's an excellent idea.'

'What?' Felix shrieked.

I started eating again. He could wait a few seconds, the little toerag. But I gave in soon enough. 'Nothing much. We thought we'd try out the indoor go-karts. Kyla and her auntie are going to come too.'

It's a wonder his eyes didn't fall out of their sockets and land in his porridge. 'All of us? Me too? Can I drive one? Can I really? Mum?'

She gave her eyes a scrub and dredged up a smile. 'Yes, darling. You can drive one.'

I swear that kid's feet didn't touch the ground for the rest of the morning. His mother could well have regretted that he was into talking now, because every two minutes he'd ask, 'Is it time yet? Can we go now?'

MY MATES WERE already there when we arrived. Erica took one glance at the track and looked like she might faint.

I beckoned Felix over. 'Listen, mate. I'm going to drive a few slow laps. You follow me. Follow my line through the corners. Do exactly what I do and don't worry about the other buggers. Okay?'

He nodded, eyes on full beam. 'Will we pass other karts?'

I grinned at him. 'Let's just get the cornering right. First things first, kind of thing.'

'Okay!' He buzzed off to get kitted up.

I reckon Dad was just as excited as Felix was, but he

was trying to keep the brake on it for Erica's sake. If she actually got into one of the karts it'd be a miracle.

The last group of drivers finished their session, and it was our turn for the track. We got the briefing and the instructions about how to drive the karts, then we were off. Dad waited behind to make sure Felix got started, and by the time I came round again there was no sign of either of them, or of Erica, so I figured the little rat must be doing okay. I caught him up, passed him, and we did five slow circuits with me in front to guide him round the corners. The others kept whipping past and yahooing as they went.

The sixth lap, I lifted my hand to signal to Felix and accelerated. He'd either be okay, or he wouldn't.

I got down to serious racing. Kyla was leading — no surprise there — but Joanna was right behind her, with Dad poised to sneak past her. James was leading my group of mates, followed by Ginnie, then Colin, with Nina and Silas trailing them. Erica was a couple of kart lengths back and seemed to be intent on keeping the gap. Felix was out on his own and, by the look of it, he was doing all right.

My mates were so easy to pick off in the corners, it was pathetic. I looked ahead — Joanna had to have raced before. By the time I caught her, Dad had got past her. I ducked through as she came out of a corner, then it was off after Dad.

He was a cunning old bugger and hard to get past. He was up there, niggling away at Kyla too. The three of us circled in formation for a couple of laps before we caught Felix. I passed Dad when he took his mind off the game to watch him. Didn't catch Kyla, though. She knew it was me behind her and no way was she going to let me through. We lapped Erica and the bunch of five, but Kyla held the lead. We got the *time up* signal. I moved out beside her to race her to the finish. She won by a nose.

Dad came in next, followed by Joanna. Kyla and I started to laugh. Felix had passed Nina and Silas. Erica was last off the track, but she arrived in time to watch Felix scramble out of his kart, whip off the helmet and see his huge grin. She heard him too — the whole place probably did. 'That was *awesome*! I passed Silas and I passed Nina. Did you see that, Archie? Mum — isn't it *awesome*!'

Dad, with a swift look at Erica's less than ecstatic face, said, 'Good work, my man. Not many people get past two karts and especially not their first time out.'

Erica gave him a hug and he didn't notice she was trying her best not to bawl. Joanna gave her a thoughtful look, slipped an arm round her and said, 'You and I need a good cup of tea, Erica. You others go and amuse yourselves.'

Dad came with us and we spent the rest of the afternoon playing snooker, watching other karters and eating. At some point, Dad drifted back to Erica. By the time we left, she was looking calmer. Not happy, though. More like resigned — as if she'd accepted that her kid was going to race.

'She okay?' I asked Joanna on the way home in her car.

'Give her time. She'll get there. I pointed out that he's going to scare her no matter what he does.'

'It must be hard for her, seeing what people do to themselves,' Kyla said.

'You drive a mean race,' I said to Joanna. I needed to

be distracted from the image of the broken skull Erica had stuck in my head.

She said, 'But I'm not at all competitive.'

Kyla laughed all the rest of the way home.

We went out that night, just the two of us. Her last night. We ate at a cheap and cheerful place in town, then wandered along the waterfront for a bit, before finishing the evening with a movie.

Joanna picked me up early the next afternoon to go the airport. When Kyla got in the back to sit with me, Joanna turned herself into a tour guide with a fairly pointed commentary. 'And now we're passing Te Papa where, if you're not careful, you will see plenty of exhibits of the perils of passion.'

The other one that stuck in my mind was her comment on the Wellington sign. 'Up there on the hill is the Wellington Blown Away sign. It's really a message. Love blows away on the wind, is what it says.'

In spite of the sarcasm, she took her time parking the car so we could say goodbye properly. She wouldn't let me stay to watch the plane take off, though. 'Well, you can if you want, Archie. The bus goes regularly.'

For a moment, I considered it. But I'd dented my bank account during the past week and the bus cost money. Joanna drove me home. I watched the city pass by and felt the ache of missing Kyla.

CHAPTER TWENTY-FOUR

THE LAST FRIDAY of the holidays I jumped on a train and went to visit my mother. It was a risk, because I hadn't let her know her I was coming. But, as far as I could tell, she and her man never strayed far from their land.

I sat on the train and tried to work out exactly what I wanted to ask her. No, bugger it, I knew what I wanted to ask: *Tell me the truth about why you ran off and left me.* I wasn't sure how you asked a question like that. What it amounted to was that we didn't know each other well. In my head there was a list of information about her:

> into organic gardening
> lives with Anselm
> has dark hair and eyes like me
> hates motor sport of all kind
> emails me every week
> sends me useless birthday presents
> always wants me to go to her for Christmas

It wasn't much to know about your mother. I knew I should take more notice of her emails but, actually, I just skimmed over them to make sure she wasn't dying or anything. To be honest, they were pretty boring. She tried. That was important, I guess.

I walked the couple of ks from the station. Turned off the road into the long driveway leading up to the house, and caught sight of her working in amongst some bushes. I vaulted the fence.

'Hi, Mum!'

She straightened up and a big smile broke out. 'Archie!' She started running towards me. No doubt about it, she was pleased to see me. She hugged me, wiped at her eyes and said, 'I can't believe it! You're here! Come into the house and I'll make you a drink. Anselm will be thrilled to see you, too.'

I held back. 'Mum, I want to talk to you first. Ask you a few things.'

She stopped walking, hugged her arms around her body, then nodded. 'All right. Come into the shed.' She led the way into a shed full of gardening gear. She pulled a couple of stools out from under a bench. 'Sit down.' She looked straight at me. It was uncanny — it was like looking at my own eyes in a mirror. 'You want to know why I abandoned you.' It wasn't a question.

I frowned, trying to untangle my thoughts. 'I didn't ever feel abandoned. I just . . . look, I know you and Dad both say it was nothing to do with me. But I've still got this idea in the back of my head. Would you have stayed if I hadn't got into karting?'

There it was. Out in the open. Plain and simple.

Her eyes filled with tears. *Oh great. Visit your mum and make her cry.*

'No. That had nothing to do with it. I promise you.'

Yeah, I'd heard that before. Still didn't believe it. And it didn't answer the other big question. 'Why didn't you take me with you? Don't get me wrong — Dad's brilliant. We have the best life. But usually . . .'

'Mothers take the kids with them,' she finished for me. She smiled at me — it was a creaky sort of smile but it was better than the tears. 'Do you know how old I am, Archie?'

What? My face got hot because I didn't have a clue. I knew how old Dad was. Forty-four. His birthday was Guy Fawke's day. I said, 'Your birthday's in April. The twenty-third.' I always sent her a card and rang her up. If I could think what to get, I'd buy her a present too, which meant she got something about every third year. But I didn't know how old she was.

'I'm thirty-three. I was just two years older than you are now when I had you.'

I was still getting my head around that when she went on, 'I'm not excusing myself. Lots of girls have babies young, and lots of them do a great job of being mums. But I couldn't do it. I tried, and I tried to believe that Bill was my soulmate. I was in a pretty bad state. We went to counselling, but all that did was show up the gap between us.'

This was so different from the story in my head. Freaky. I kept my mouth shut, waiting for the rest of it.

'To cut a miserable story short — we put you in day care while I got a job. It was such a relief.'

'The job, or getting rid of me?'

She frowned at me. 'Try and understand, Archie. Think how you'd cope with a baby. I was terrified of babies. I was horrified by what I'd let happen to my life. When other people saw this . . . object . . . they'd coo and say things like *Isn't he gorgeous! You must be so proud. He's adorable.* I felt useless.'

'So you walked out?'

'After another five years. Yes. I left. I met Anselm at a course in organic gardening. Six months later, I went to live with him and told Bill I wasn't coming back.'

'Did he mind?' I had no memory of any of this.

She winced. 'He minded all right. He was very bitter. Said some nasty things, and said he'd fight me every step of the way if I tried to take you with me.'

I stared at her. None of that sounded like the father I knew. Bitter? Nasty?

She looked sad. 'Divorce can bend people out of shape, Archie. I didn't try to contact him. I knew if I kept quiet he'd get back in touch eventually. And he did. He was sorry he'd said the bad stuff, but he was firm about keeping you.'

I had a feeling that she was working herself up to the crunch point, to tell me the thing I possibly didn't want to hear. I was right.

She looked at me as she said it. 'I didn't fight for you, Archie. I didn't fight because I knew I didn't want to be a mother. Every time I thought about it, it felt like a weight falling on me. I'm sorry. I'm really sorry, but that's the truth of it. I've taken good care never to get pregnant again.'

She shut up then and we sat in silence with our thoughts. Don't know what hers were, but mine were tearing around in all directions. All I could think of to say was, 'Thanks for telling me the truth, Mum. It's good to know the whole story.' It was so different from the story I'd had in my head.

'You know, Archie — I was so lucky I had the sense to get pregnant to a man as good as Bill. I'd been leading a wild life till he rescued me from a fight on the street one night. He took me back to his flat and cleaned the blood off me. And I just stayed on. We didn't get together until I'd been there for several months, but he kept an eye on me and it was a real novelty to have somebody look out for me. I stopped the drinking. Didn't go looking for drugs. We sort of drifted into a relationship, and when I got pregnant we got married and moved into a place of our own.'

'Then I came along and spoiled it all.'

She pulled her mouth down. 'Babies do that, Archie. They cry, they sick up and they smell bad. I tried to pretend you were a puppy, but it didn't help.'

I couldn't help it. I laughed. 'So what you're saying is that it was bloody lucky for me that Dad kept me?'

But she shuddered. 'I hate to think what I'd have done if he hadn't, Archie. I really do.' She stood up. 'Can I get you something to eat and drink now? Or do you want to run for the hills?'

'It's sweet,' I said. 'Food would be good.'

We went to the house, collecting Anselm along the way. He wasn't a bad bloke, he just wasn't my sort of bloke. As we ate sandwiches and drank tea we made polite conversation, and I understood finally that I'd have been a miserable kid if I'd had to grow up with him as my father, because nothing he talked about was the slightest bit interesting to me. They asked me about school, but they didn't ask about the karting.

Mum drove me to the station. Along the way she said, 'Is it working out with Erica?'

'Yeah. They get on good. Felix is okay too.'

'I'm glad. Your dad's a good man.' She pulled up, but put her hand on my arm to stop me getting out. 'Archie — you've got a girlfriend? Be careful. Look after her, I mean. You don't want to be a father before you're ready.'

'Jeez, Mum!'

She let me go. We did the goodbye kiss thing, and I jumped on to the train with a lot to think about. My mother had been a drunk, druggie wild child. Maybe Dad knew what he was doing when he got together with Erica this time round.

CHAPTER TWENTY-FIVE

AT DINNER THAT night I said, as casually as I could, 'I went to visit Mum today.'

'She'd be pleased,' Dad said. 'What brought that on?'

'Curiosity.'

'Ah. And?'

'All good. Straightened out a few things in my head.' I was aware Felix was staring at me, and that Erica was trying to look like she didn't want to know the full story.

It was obvious I didn't have to spell out to Dad what those 'few things' might be. 'If I'd let her take you, you'd have had a mother and a father.' The way he said it made me wonder if that was a question he'd always had lurking at the back of his mind too.

'Shit, Dad. I'd have died of boredom. There's not a lot of excitement in caterpillars and cabbages.'

He relaxed, gave me a grin. End of conversation. Fine by me.

SCHOOL STARTED AGAIN, but my attention was on club day at the end of the first week, followed by the fourth Challenge meeting a week later. This one would be at the Bay of Plenty track. Erica told Felix he could go to both events, but she turned down Dad's invitation to come with us to club day.

I spent as much time as I could working on my kart to make sure it was in top condition. Felix helped. Pre-Erica, Dad would have done most of the job himself, but I told him to hang out with her, we could always give him a yell if we needed him. So, one night, they went out to dinner. That wasn't exactly what I'd had in mind.

They were home in time to do the bed routine with Felix, though, so I disappeared to put in some time catching up with my mates on Facebook. Well, well — what a surprise. Craig was shooting his mouth off again about Silver.

I hear Silver Adams got a warning from the stewards for dangerous driving. She needs to be banned. End of story.

I wrote: *Give it a rest, Craig! How's the hunt for a new mechanic going?*

Other drivers added their bits: *If you can't stand the heat, stay off the track.*

Handle the jandal.

He's right tho. We don't want dangerous drivers. Bad for everyone.

I left them to it and talked to Kyla. I told her about Mum.

'Far out! Are you okay about it, Archie?'

'Yeah. I am. I reckon she got herself into a life that didn't fit her. It'd be like me trying to fit in with her life now.' I shook my head. 'That would be bad, believe me.'

CLUB DAY ARRIVED full of wind and skittering rain. The gossip out at the track was about Craig. His father had got him a new mechanic but nobody seemed to know any more than that. Typical Craig to give out just enough info to make people curious and keep them guessing.

I put him out of my mind. My task was to drive as smoothly as I could and to practise my passing.

Dad wrote down the stats for each race and we made adjustments to try to get as much speed from the kart as we could. Felix shadowed Dad, taking in every scrap of info and running errands. He was turning out to have a brain too, and initiative. Like he disappeared mid-morning, then came back with tea and sandwiches for both of us.

'Thanks, mate,' Dad said. 'But where did you get the money?'

'I said you'd pay later. And I ate a muffin but I only had a drink of water.'

I had to laugh. Felix could have a lesson or two on booking things up in Dad's name coming up fairly soon. The drink and the food were an excellent idea, though.

We finished the day with the kart as well set up as we could get it. Back home, Felix helped me with taking it apart and cleaning it. We spent the next three evenings going over it and checking everything. Dad put the hours in as well. It wasn't much fun for Erica, but she didn't say anything.

I skyped Kyla on Wednesday night — there wouldn't be time the next day, because we were getting away straight after school. I told her how much I wished she could compete in the Challenge, but she just laughed at me. 'I'd have beaten you and you'd have to pretend you were proud of me.'

I didn't bother arguing. Not when we both knew I'd have been gutted. Instead we talked about how the internet was full of rumours about who Craig's new mechanic was. He'd be ecstatic.

At school the next day I got the word from three of my teachers that they would like some of my attention. Nina didn't help. She passed me a note in English saying, *I've got an amped up, supercharged hex this time. Craig is toast.*

Dad and Felix picked me up at the end of the day, but we made it to Dannevirke before I got the text from Craig: *Track looking good. My mechanics set up kart already.*

I read it out.

'He's doing that . . . that . . . mess with your head thing again,' Felix said.

'Yep. That's it, mate. Psychological warfare.'

'I think he's a mutant,' said my step-brother.

Dad and I cracked up.

WE WERE STAYING with Gran and Grandad in Tauranga, so there was no problem hitting the track early. They had the morning routine timed to perfection.

Craig had his base set up already — or rather, his mechanic had set it up. As soon as he saw us, he ambled over, getting in the way while we put up our tent and organised things.

Bugger him — he'd be waiting for me to ask about his mechanic. Let him wait.

Dad must have got sick of him, too, because he started

giving him jobs: 'Craig, grab hold of the groundsheet, would you. Straighten it out. Good. Now can you take the end of the bench? We'll move it back slightly.'

It worked. He melted away like butter on a barbie.

Felix, meantime, went out on an info-gathering mission. He was back in ten minutes. 'Jack said the new mechanic is Gus from Australia. Sel says Gus got the sack from his last job. Tama says he's an ace mechanic even if he did get fired.'

'Good work, my man. You ever heard of the guy, Dad?'

He shook his head. 'No, nothing. It'll be interesting to see how the two of them get along.'

Badly, I hoped, but as the day went on it looked more and more like Craig and Gus were best mates.

'Bugger,' said Lewis. 'Much better for us if they hate each other.'

'Craig alert!' Tama said. 'The great man himself is coming to talk to us.'

We watched him stroll towards us, all casual and in control. 'Hi, guys. Dad's here. Anyone interested in taking a look at the Audi?'

Stupid question. We all went and we all drooled. No doubt about it — that was one classy piece of machinery. Mr Bateman did the decent thing, though, and showed us the engine and let each of us sit in the driver's seat. A streak of pure envy shot through me. Sometimes, it'd be quite nice to have money to throw around.

Felix and I went back to our tent. 'You have to beat him, Archie. He's a big fat skite.'

'I'll do my best, mate. Promise you that.'

But when I got out on the track for practice, the kart wasn't responding a hundred per cent. I couldn't get enough acceleration coming out of the corners. Had to laugh when I came back in, though — there were Dad and Grandad both standing with one hand on a hip and the other propping up the chin. And Felix was doing exactly the same.

'Gripped up, is it?' Dad asked.

'Yeah. Real slow off the corners.' I got out and we took the kart back to our tent.

'What can we do?' Felix asked. 'Can we fix it? Is it the tyre pressures?'

'No, won't be that,' Grandad said. 'It'll be something else to do with the set-up.'

'Let's try swapping the back axle,' Dad said. We had a standard one on.

'Hard or soft?' Grandad asked.

We decided to give the hard one a try first. It was better. Much faster coming out of the corners and the kart no longer felt like it was sticking to the track. It wasn't perfect, though.

All through the day we kept tweaking things, making small adjustments, but still it wasn't a hundred per cent. By the time practice ended, I was a full half second under the track record.

Craig was strutting around, wearing his *I'm gonna be on pole* expression. The trouble was, he was probably right.

Grandad watched him. 'Cock of the dung heap, that one. Don't worry, Archie. We'll have a think about your set-up overnight. See if we can get it perfect.'

CHAPTER TWENTY-SIX

I WAS TENSE as I lined up for the next day's tuning run. Nobody'd had a brainwave overnight about what might be wrong. But I absolutely wanted a faster qualifying time than Craig — and everybody else.

'Relax, Archie,' Grandad said. 'You'll cock up big time if you don't.'

And get a big-time bollocking from him as well. I slid into my seat, pulled on my helmet, and shut him and the world out. Focused. Relaxed. Alert. Patient.

I drove with my mind on automatic. The kart felt okay. Not a hundred per cent but good enough. When I came back in, Dad and Grandad suggested making a slight change in my seat position. 'It might just make the difference,' Dad said. 'Distribute your weight differently. Okay?'

'Might as well try.'

As soon as I got up to speed in the first qualifier, I could tell they'd sorted the problem. Good. I got myself into a clear space on the track, then set about knocking the fractions of seconds off my lap times.

When we came into the pits after the second qualifier, Craig asked as usual, 'What's your best time, Archie?'

'Half a second faster than yours.'

'You wish.'

I watched him walk away with Gus. Interesting. Craig actually had a hand on the trolley — could have even been helping push it.

We'd arrived back at our own tent when Felix came tearing in. 'The man's putting up the times, Archie.'

The two of us hurried over to the notice board. Josh and Craig were already there. Lewis, Sel, Jack and Ollie joined us on the way.

'Oops,' Jack said, 'looks like His Majesty isn't pleased.'

We watched as Craig thumped his fist on the board. When he saw us, he hauled out a grin. 'A hundredth of a second. Nothing in it.'

From that, I figured I was on pole. Craig was on two, Lewis on three, Ollie on four, Josh on five, Tama on six, Sel on twelve and Jack was back on eighteen.

'Silver's on thirteen,' Sel said. 'Not bad.'

'She won't get in our way,' Josh said.

'Speak for yourself,' Jack said. 'She'll be a problem for me. No mistake.'

'Only if you get past five people,' Sel said.

'And stay on the track,' Lewis said.

Jack just laughed. All he wanted to do was drive flat out. If he stayed on the track, that was a bonus. If he managed to pass somebody, it was like he'd won the entire series. He was lucky that his old man was rich enough and crazy enough to indulge him.

Felix helped me push my kart on to pole for the heat. I slid into my seat and into my own world. *Focus. Drive your heart out.*

Craig jumped the start. Not enough to make the stewards black flag him, but enough to damn near grab the inside. Feckin' cheat! I fed him a wheel, hitting his rear inside wheel with my front outside one. He dived off the track just enough for me to get through. *Two can play rough, old mate.*

I held the lead the entire race. Craig might have been right behind me but I shut him out of my mind and just drove. I crossed the line .25 of a second ahead of Lewis. Craig came in fifth.

He didn't come near me for the rest of the afternoon. My friends and I watched the other heats. Craig watched with his new best buddy, Gus the mechanic.

That night I told Dad and Grandad about Craig's jumped start.

Felix yelped, 'He *cheated*?'

'You could protest,' Dad said.

'I'd rather beat him,' I said.

'Fine, if you can do it without damaging your kart,' Grandad said. 'If you can't, then we protest.'

But I didn't want to beat Craig by protesting. I wanted to beat him on the track.

WE WOKE THE next morning to a sunny Bay of Plenty day. 'You can see why we love Tauranga,' Gran said as we settled ourselves on the deck to eat breakfast.

I didn't chat. My head was busy going over the track. I was concentrating, too, on how to make sure Craig didn't get ahead of me if — or more likely *when* — he jumped the start. I wanted to win that second heat to make sure I got pole for the pre-final.

At the track, we went through the normal routines

of ensuring everything was tight, fuelling the engine and running it to warm it up. Before we set out for the grid, Grandad put his hand on my shoulder. 'Drive your own race, Archie.'

Felix was more direct — and, actually, I liked his advice better. 'Beat that cheating scumbag, Archie.'

'I'll do my best, mate.'

It was a relief, though, to put on my helmet and shut out the world.

The starter counted us down for the rolling lap. We went round twice, warming our engines and tyres. As we approached the start line for the third time, every nerve was firing on alert.

Craig accelerated before the red lights went out. He dived across from the outside, intending to force me into second place so that I'd have to follow him round the bend. But I held my line. The nose of my kart clipped the back of his, but I was expecting it and he wasn't. The force threw him off the track, and I didn't hang about to ask about the state of his health.

But my kart hadn't come out of the encounter unscathed. As the heat went on, it became slower and less responsive coming out of the corners. Lewis passed me, then Craig got through. *Don't let anyone else through.* I pushed the boundaries as much as the kart would let me, but Josh snuck through on the final turn. I came in fourth.

Dad, Grandad and Felix whipped the kart on to the trolley the moment I came off the scales after the weigh-in. The three of them ran with it back to our base, with Dad and Grandad firing questions at me.

'What's it doing?'

'You want to swap the axle again?'

'Could be the axle stubs. Quite a bump you gave young Craig.'

'Yeah,' I said. 'He jumped the start. Again.'

'Quite the sportsman,' Grandad said.

'He's a dirty cheat!' said Felix.

'We don't worry about him,' Dad said. 'We drive our own race, and we don't cheat.'

'I could put glue in his fuel tank,' Felix said.

'Got any glue handy?' Dad asked.

Felix shook his head.

'We'd better get busy then,' Grandad said.

I ate the lunch Gran gave me without noticing too much what it was. She didn't mind — she was used to karters. Dad and Grandad tightened things, checked every part and discovered the sprocket wheel had a ding in it. 'Bloody lucky you didn't throw the chain, Archie,' Dad said.

'Would a ding slow me down on the corners, though?'

Grandad shrugged. 'Wouldn't help. But I think there's something else going on. Buggered if I know what.'

Great.

LEWIS WAS ON pole for the pre-final. Craig was beside him on two, I was on three and Josh on four.

As we walked back from the notice board, I said to Lewis, 'Watch out for our old mate. He's taken to jumping the start.'

'For real? Thanks for the warning,' Lewis said.

It was time to get into our karts, time to settle down and focus on the race ahead.

I used the rolling laps to test the feel of the set-up. It seemed better. I hoped it was.

The lights went out. I put my foot down, hot on the tails of Craig and Lewis. Craig dived across to cut Lewis off — before the lights went out. Lewis bashed into the back of his kart, and they both spun off on to the grass. I nipped through to take the lead.

My kart felt better. Perfect, in fact. My mechanics must've fixed the problem when they went over it at lunch break. I kept my mind on the job, driving smoothly, driving consistently and keeping out of trouble.

I crossed the finish line with Lewis and Ollie battling for second behind me. Where was Craig? Truthfully, I didn't much care. I'd beaten him and that was what mattered.

We cruised into the pits, put the karts over the scales without any problems — not that there would be. We weren't cheats. Speaking of which, Craig got himself out of his seat, tugged off his helmet, then yelled at Silver, 'I'm reporting you! Deliberate blocking. They'll ban you. I'll make sure they do.'

He might as well have been yelling at a wall, for all the reaction she gave him.

But I'd had enough of him. 'Jumping the start isn't in the rules, either.'

He swung around, his fist bunched. 'That's a bloody lie, Archie Barrington. I don't cheat.'

'You jumped the pre-final,' Lewis said.

'You jumped both the heats,' I said.

'Put in a protest if you're so sure,' Craig said.

Lewis looked at me, and I nodded. 'Do it again, and we will. Both of us.'

Craig stormed off, leaving Gus to get his kart on to the trolley and back to their base.

Sel said, 'He's changed. So different from how he was last year.'

'Yeah,' Ollie said, 'he's always been up himself. But never this bad.'

'Silver did good,' Jack said. 'I was behind her the whole race. She was a bit loose, but nothing dangerous.'

'Where did Craig come?' I asked. But nobody knew. We had to wait for the results to be posted.

'Twentieth!' Josh said. 'No wonder he was pissed.'

'And look at his grid for the final! Ten.'

But we weren't looking at that. Our eyes were glued to the number beside him — 47. Silver Adams. Fate had a weird sense of humour. Or it could be sense of justice.

Back in our tent, I asked, 'What happened to Craig?'

'Got his knickers in a twist is my guess,' Grandad said. 'Can't handle the pressure. Fine when he's winning. Sulks when it doesn't go his way.'

'Completely lost his focus,' Dad said.

'He's a bloody shitty driver,' said Felix.

Dad rolled his eyes, handed him a spanner and set him to work.

The final was a good scrap between Lewis and me. He got past me once when I went too wide and left the door open. It took me two entire laps before I snuck through on the inside.

'You bloody handed him that corner on a plate, Archie!' Grandad growled when I returned to my crew. 'Bloody careless.'

'I know. But did you notice — I got past him again.'

Grandad just snorted. Dad winked at me, but Felix leapt to my defence. 'He won! He drove good and he won. You're mean!'

Which meant that while we packed up, Dad and I had

to explain to Felix that Grandad was a big softie. 'His bark is worse than his bite,' Dad said.

Felix looked bewildered, so I said, 'He yells when he cares about you. It's a good sign. You'll see, he'll yell at you too.'

'I can bloody hear you,' Grandad said. 'I'm not deaf and I'm not dead.'

'Time for prize-giving,' Gran said.

Again, Craig didn't bother turning up. I made a speech, accepted the trophy and was very, very happy. But I knew this would be the result that Craig would drop, which meant that if I dropped my Tokoroa result then we still had exactly the same ranking — with him one miserable point ahead of me.

We were down to the final two races of the series now. The next one was in Auckland, Craig's home turf. The last one would be in Rotorua. Craig would know both of those tracks better than I did.

CHAPTER TWENTY-SEVEN

THERE WAS A month between the Bay of Plenty event and the Auckland one. Teachers have no hearts. They handed out assignments and got manic about deadlines.

'Get the work done, Archie. And do it well,' was Mr Taylor's advice as he dished out yet another load of work. 'If you do get to Portugal, you'll miss your NCEA exams. You'll need good results from the rest of the year because they'll be used to assess what your mark is.'

That aspect of things hadn't been high on my radar. I'd kept the work up, but I couldn't say I'd gone hard out. Not to worry. As long as I got enough credits to get through Level 1. I did the assignments, did the homework and spent all my free moments working on the kart. I even said no to a party my mates were planning on going to one Friday night — time was precious and I had too much to do.

Club day at my home track at Kaitoke was the week before Auckland. We decided to use the back-up engine that day to give it a run. Dad, Felix and I spent all of Saturday preparing my kart. Erica was working but she didn't suggest sending Felix to his carer's for the day. And she must have been expecting the question he asked at dinner that night. 'Mum, I can go tomorrow, can't I?'

I figured she'd have to have a heart of steel to ignore that pleading puppy dog look. True, she didn't look happy, but she said, 'Yes, dear. You can go.' Then, while he was still bouncing round in his seat, she looked at Dad and me. 'I'm trusting you both to keep him safe.'

Get real, Erica — shit happens. Don't you know that yet?

But Dad held her hand and said, 'Of course we will, darling. You know that.'

Darling. Yerk. I rolled my eyes at Felix. He giggled.

Erica had left for work by the time we got on the road. Up at the track, Felix raced around, happy, focused and actually quite helpful. He disappeared when the cadet class was called, but we didn't stress about it. He knew where he wasn't allowed to go, and he knew Dad meant it when he said he'd leave him behind next time if he got up to mischief.

We had the kart on the trolley, warming up the engine, when he came back. 'Bill, am I old enough to race in the cadet class?'

Dad shut the engine down. 'Yes, you are. But your mum would have to agree, or it's no go.'

The kid didn't say anything more, but by the look on his face there could be storms ahead.

My race was called. I intended to work on smoothness, cornering and passing, rather than getting hung up on winning. Huh! Who was I kidding — winning was what it was all about.

The pre-determined randomised grid starts gave me plenty of opportunities to practise passing. The final race of the day, I was at the back but worked my way up to take the lead and win. A good day. I hoped it was a good omen for Auckland.

BACK HOME, WE got the kart taken apart before Erica arrived from work. Then Felix and I did the cleaning while she and Dad cooked dinner.

'You're turning out to be quite useful, mate,' I said.

'D'you reckon Mum'll let me drive?'

I shrugged. 'She's not keen, Felix.'

He put some elbow grease into cleaning the back axle. 'I'm going to ask her anyway.'

He did. At dinner. She downed her knife and fork, took a huge breath and said clearly and slowly, 'No, Felix. Not now. Not ever. Please don't ask again.'

'You're a mean, stinky mummy. So there!' He twisted out of his chair, knocked it flat and ran out of the room.

Erica dropped her head into her hands and groaned. 'I knew this would happen. I *knew* it.'

I finished my dinner. It was good and I wasn't going to leave it. Nobody said anything for the rest of the meal, though. I cleared the table and shut myself in the kitchen. Then I went in search of the mobile temper tantrum. He was crying on his bed.

'Shut it, Felix. We've got work to do. The kitchen. Now.' I went out. He'd either come or he wouldn't. I set the remains of his dinner to one side and started cleaning up.

He drooped in after about five minutes. 'She's *mean*.'

'So you said. Listen, mate. You've got to learn to handle disappointment. Throwing a tantrum — shit, that's what Craig does.' I pointed at his plate. 'There's the rest of your dinner.'

'It's cold.'

'Poor little Felix. Doesn't know how to warm up

his dinner.' I kept on with stacking the dishwasher and didn't look his way.

I heard a big sniff, then he shoved the plate in the microwave and hit a button. I grinned at him and got a wobbly smile back. He scoffed the rest of his dinner while I finished clearing up.

'But Archie, I really do want to race.' He did the puppy dog look real well.

'I know you do, mate. Looks like you might have to wait till you're eighteen though.'

'That's *old*!'

I laughed at him, then told him a few of the cold, hard facts, starting with showing him the bruising along my ribs and on the inside of my knees. 'Racing throws you around. You wear the rib protectors but it doesn't stop all the bruising. And you're always bruising your knees where they knock against the fuel tank. After a day's racing, you'll be stiff and sore — aching in every muscle. G-forces aren't kind to bodies.'

He was suspicious. 'But you're not sore now.'

'Sure I am. No point in going on about it. That's what happens when you race.'

He thought about that for a moment. 'I don't care. I still want to race.'

'Well, I wouldn't mention it again right now, if I were you.'

I had homework to do and Kyla to catch up with. I shut myself in my room, raced through some science revision, then settled into chatting with Kyla, who updated me on the Facebook gossip that I'd been too busy to look at. 'Have a look, Archie. Craig's come out with a big fat apology to Silver.'

I logged in and there it was: *Hey, Silver — really sorry*

I yelled at you. Just got a bit carried away.

She, of course, hadn't replied.

'What d'you think?' Kyla asked.

'He's doing it to look good. A public apology — it's for the rest of us, not for Silver.'

'Just what I thought,' Kyla said.

She also told me that a couple of the South Island competitors had dropped out. They knew they couldn't win, and it was too expensive to travel twice more to the North Island when they had no chance of taking the prize.

We only chatted for half an hour before the tiredness from the day hit me. Kyla laughed. 'Bed time for Archie.'

I reckon I was asleep before I got my head on the pillow. Only a week to Auckland — Craig's home track.

CHAPTER TWENTY-EIGHT

AT SCHOOL THAT week my mind was on the racing ahead — and my mates dropped in the odd comment about how they were expecting a postcard every day once I got to Portugal. And Nina said, 'Do I still need to keep my hex active?'

'Absolutely,' I said. 'Big-time hexing needed.'

Ginnie slapped my arm. 'Don't encourage her. She's starting to believe in it.'

Colin said, 'You bloody shouldn't, Nina. Look what happened Saturday.'

'It's not my fault you lost! You played rotten — the whole team. Not even a titanium hex could fix that.'

'Hung over,' James said. 'Good party, though.'

Lucky I hadn't gone. Dad might have had something to say if I'd got pissed.

WE LEFT MIDDAY Thursday — more time off school for Felix and me. I reckon he really would have stowed away if Erica had said he couldn't go. But she seemed to have got used to him tagging along with us.

When he dozed off in the heat of the van, I said to Dad, 'Will she ever let him race?'

'Hard to tell. She's hoping he'll be happy with just watching.'

I snorted. That kid was busting to race.

'One step at a time, Archie. She's come a long way already.'

'So has her kid.'

Dad nodded. 'He sure has. That's the only reason she can get her head around letting him come and watch.'

It was a long drive to Auckland. I passed time by texting Kyla and listening to music with my headphones on. Felix was bound to start asking *Are we there yet?* and I figured Dad could handle that. When we pulled up at the motel, several of my mates were already there — Ollie, Josh and Lewis. No sign of Sel or Jack, but they could be at a different motel.

At the track next morning, the kart felt good and we didn't need to do any tweaking, so I was able to concentrate on learning the track. I'd raced on it before, but not as often as Craig had. The way he was strolling around, you'd think he owned the whole outfit. He kept well clear of Silver, though.

I had an interesting encounter with her during practice just before lunch. I came up behind her, didn't tap the back of her kart — asking for trouble to do that — but she knew there was someone chasing her. We came up to the top corner, I outbraked her, but she jabbed at the steering, locked up the brakes and took the corner sideways. I avoided the crash by going wide on to the grass. *Kamikaze Silver strikes again.* I made sure I kept a distance of half the track between us after that.

Craig was in my ear as soon as we came off the track. 'See? She needs to be banned. I saw what she did. I'll back you up. We'll go to the stewards right now.'

'You please yourself,' I said, 'but I'm going where the food is.'

His face went red. 'You'll be sorry. Don't come whining to me, that's all.'

'I'll try not to. Come on. The canteen's calling.' I'd taken a couple of steps before he caught me up. I changed the subject to get his mind off Silver. 'How's the new mechanic working out?'

Good choice of topic. He gushed about the wonders of Gus the Mechanic as we walked, as we bought our food, and he was still at it when we sat down.

After the lunch break, I used the practice time to push the limits, to find out where they were — went off a few times. Worth it.

The next morning I did the tuning run, then before the qualifiers we took off the practice tyres and bolted on the wheels fitted with my sponsor's new ones. I was glad of that sponsorship. Craig didn't need it, and it was saving Dad and me a heap of money over the series.

Gran texted to say they'd arrived and where were we? 'I'll go and find them,' Felix said, and raced off.

'Useful kid,' Dad said.

The three of them came back, Felix carrying Gran's folding chair. We got the hugging and kissing out of the way, then Dad, Felix and Grandad came down to the grid with me for the qualifier. 'Good luck, son,' said Dad.

'Beat the other bastards,' said Grandad.

'Stay on the track, Archie,' said Felix.

Good advice.

I was pleased with my time for the qualifier. Craig might have been faster, but there'd be nothing much in it if he was. Bummer if he got pole by a miserable fraction of a second, though.

'Happy with that?' Dad asked.

'Yeah. All good.'

Craig came over as we were lifting the kart on to the trolley. 'Going out for the second run, Archie? You'll need to if you want to beat my time.'

'That so? What'd you do?'

He did his usual trick of exaggerating.

I laughed. The time was a second faster than mine. No way.

'Don't say I didn't warn you.' He ambled off.

I frowned, staring at his back. That was something new. A whole second? Nah. That couldn't be right — Craig and his games. Who needed them?

He was down at the notice board, ready and waiting, when the steward posted the times and the grid positions for the heats. So was Josh. He stared at the list, said something to Craig, then raced over to meet the rest of us.

'Craig's on pole. He's a whole second faster than you, Archie.'

That stopped us dead. 'Sure you read that right?' Ollie asked.

'Yeah. I did. Unfortunately.'

'This I have to see with my own two eyes,' said Lewis.

So did I — but there it was: Craig Bateman on pole, with me beside him, a whole second slower.

'Shit. The bloody day's going to be a walk-over,' Sel said.

Not if I could help it.

But by the end of the first heat I was worried. I pushed the limits, driving to the absolute max of the kart and my skill. Craig crossed the finish line a length ahead of me. What the hell was happening?

I shook my head at him as we slid out of our seats. 'Mate — you've got wings. Well done, you bastard.'

He laughed. 'Never mind, Archie. A good second place — nothing to be ashamed of.'

'How about you give us lessons?' Ollie asked, only half joking.

Craig strutted across to Gus, slung an arm round his shoulders and said, 'It's my brilliant mechanic. Ask him for lessons.' He actually smirked at Dad.

Dad didn't react — just got on with the job of lifting my kart on to the trolley, helped by Grandad and Felix.

Back at our tent, Grandad patted my shoulder. 'It's his home track, Archie. Can make all the difference.' But I could tell he was just as puzzled as I was.

Felix popped out from behind the trolley. 'Did he cheat again, Archie? Did he jump the start again?'

I shook my head. 'No. If anything, he was a bit slow.'

Grandad said thoughtfully, 'There's other ways of cheating. He's tried one way. Doesn't mean he won't try others.' He scuffed Felix's hair. 'The young fella could be on to something here.'

'He'd be an idiot to rig the kart,' I said. 'He'd get caught at the tech check and disqualified.' You couldn't drop a DQ result — Craig knew that as well as I did. If he did get disqualified, I'd be leading the Challenge. 'He wouldn't do it.'

'He might if they put everything back to how it should be before the final,' Dad said.

'Like what, though? What could give him that sort of

advantage?' I wasn't convinced. There was too much at stake to do something that dumb and risk getting caught.

Dad and Grandad went into their thinking pose. Felix copied them. I took myself outside for some head-clearing time.

ON SUNDAY, WHILE I was sitting on the grid waiting for our second heat to start, I went over my tactics for the race. If Craig was slow off the start again, I might be able to get past and grab the inside. He'd get past me, the way he was flying round the track, but there was no point in handing him the win on a gold plate. He could bloody work for it.

The steward flagged us off. We drove the rolling laps. The second the lights went out, I accelerated. Craig was slow off the mark again, and I got through. What the hell was he playing at? Something was seriously strange. But I had a race to drive — to win if I possibly could.

I drove hard out. No messing around at eighty per cent. I gave it a hundred per cent. He passed me on the straight. On the *straight*, for hell's sake. I couldn't catch him. He was always half a kart length in front. Sometimes a whole length.

We cruised into the pits. Ollie took off his helmet. 'Okay. That's it. I'm enrolling for mechanic lessons from Gus.'

'He's gold, all right,' Lewis said. 'Any more where he came from?'

Craig smiled and strutted — very graciously. He always drove better when he was winning. He sure was driving like a pro today. I felt like a beginner.

Gran's hot soup and scones warmed me but didn't make me feel any more cheerful. 'Never mind, Archie,' she said. 'You've done your best.'

But I did mind. I minded that, realistically, I'd lost any chance of winning the Challenge. No trip to Portugal for Archie Barrington. What I minded even more was not driving as well as Craig. I'd always thought there wasn't much between us, except that I did better than he did when the going got rough.

Dad and Grandad busied themselves with checking the kart, their faces grim. Felix was sniffing back tears. I couldn't stand it — I got myself out of there.

CHAPTER TWENTY-NINE

I DROVE THAT pre-final with everything I had — pushing the limits, driving on automatic with every sense tuned to the job in hand.

Craig won by a full half second.

I took a few deep breaths and drove the slow-down lap, trying to get my head around the fact that he'd be the one winning the Challenge. After today he'd be three points ahead of me, and if he drove like this at Rotorua — goodbye Portugal.

Craig put his kart across the scales, followed by me, Ollie, then Lewis. We got out of our seats, took off the helmets, stretched out the muscles and went to meet our pit crews as normal. Except that the chief steward stepped in. 'First four karts to stay in the tech shed for a compliance check.'

'What!' Craig yelped. 'This is the pre-final, not the fecking final!' Ollie, Lewis and I stared at the steward, and then at Craig who was just about hopping with fury. 'This is ridiculous! We've never had to do this before. It's not in the rules.'

Lewis said, 'What's the problem, Craig? You've got nothing to hide. Just shut up and get it over with.'

Ollie kept his mouth shut. So did I. We'd both noticed Gus's face — red and frowning. And Craig was a touch agitated. *Cheating?* Had Dad said something to the stewards? My head was a mess. I kind of hoped Craig was cheating, but another part of me didn't want to believe it.

The steward began with my kart. He did the usual scraping of the tyres to get the samples to send away for doping analysis, but not even Craig would be dumb enough to use something on his tyres to soften them. Next, the steward ran his tape measure over my back axle. No problem. Same for Ollie, same for Lewis. Craig stamped a foot and kicked a rear wheel.

'Step back from the kart,' the steward ordered.

Craig took a step back and nearly thumped into a couple of drivers who'd just come off the scales. They took off their helmets — Jack and Silver. Craig roared at her, 'Who d'you think you're looking at? Bitch!'

She didn't drop her eyes and she stayed where she was. I wouldn't like to get on the wrong side of Silver Adams.

The steward ignored the ranting as he ran the tape over Craig's back axle. 'Thirteen millimetres too wide.' His voice was totally expressionless. 'Disqualified.'

Lewis gaped at the steward, then at Craig. 'You've been *cheating*? Jumping the start wasn't enough?'

The steward looked interested in that but didn't comment. Craig stormed out of the tech shed, followed by Gus. I should have been feeling good, but all I felt was sick.

Dad, Grandad and Felix pushed my kart back to our base. All around us, the word was spreading out in visible ripples. *Cheating? Craig?* Shock, disbelief, disgust.

But the entire place must've heard him yelling at Gus, 'It was your idea, you moron!'

'Liar! You suggested it in the first place!'

Then Mr Bateman got into the middle of it. 'Both of you. Back to the caravan. Now.'

Gus followed him, swearing and cursing. Nina's hex was small fish in comparison. Mr Bateman stopped dead, spun around and fixed his eyes on Gus. He didn't say a word, but Gus shut up. Not another squeak out of him.

Dad squeezed my shoulder. 'Nail that final, Archie. Forget about Craig. This could well be the lesson he's been needing for a good while now.'

I went off by myself for some quiet time to get my head back where it needed to be. Getting disqualified was serious. You weren't allowed to drop a DQ race from the final total. Craig wouldn't have a hope of winning the Challenge now. It was dumb to cheat, especially when he might have beaten me fair and square.

Bugger it. I didn't need to be thinking about him, or about the series. My job was to get in the head space for the next race. With Craig relegated to the back of the grid, I'd be on pole, with Ollie beside me on two

Footsteps sounded behind me. It was Ollie. 'You reckon he'll stay for the final?'

I shrugged. 'Dunno. It'd take guts to do that. He never likes being at the back of the grid either.'

We stood in silence for a bit, then Ollie said, 'Hard to stop thinking about it, eh?'

'You know what I can't understand? That extra width on the back — it shouldn't make such a difference. So why the hell was he that much faster than the rest of us?'

Ollie swore, then kicked at the ground. 'They

should've given his bloody kart the full compliance check.'

But if they'd done that, Craig wouldn't have been able to compete in the final. I wondered if that was why Mr Bateman had hustled him and Gus into the caravan. Had he been in on the scam as well? Or was he just used to springing into action when the shit hit the fan?

Not my worry. I had a final to win. Time to get back to the others and go down to the grid.

But it was impossible to stop thinking about Craig, mainly because there was no sign of him. Was he going to tough it out and race, or was he going to wimp out and run? His father might have something to say about which way the cookie would crumble. We stood around waiting for the call to start our engines, but nobody came right out and said anything. Instead, we kept glancing to where their caravan was parked, looking to see if he was going to show.

He left it till the last possible second before he came down to the grid. Didn't spare a nod for any of us. Gus wasn't with him — it was his father who helped him lift the kart off the trolley. First time for everything, I guess. Like it was the first time for Craig to be at the back of the grid in a final.

Okay, Craig. That's it. Get out of my head.

I got in my kart and did the prelim work. Focused my mind on the race, reviewed the track, worked out tactics. The starter let us go. Round we went in strict formation for the rolling laps. No problems.

I took the lead as soon as the lights gave us the signal. My plan was to stay in front, to stay on the track and not do anything stupid. This was my race to win. Ollie chased me. Lewis was close behind, hunting me down.

Josh and Sel wouldn't be far away either.

But this wasn't a race to drive at a hundred per cent. This was a take-no-risks race. A stay-on-the-track-and-win race.

The laps counted down. I held the lead, drove smoothly, drove with determination. Three laps before the end, I was aware of karts going off behind me — caught a glimpse of the tangle as I came out of the hairpin. Nothing to worry me. They were off on the grass. There was only one kart still there when I came round in the next lap: 47. Silver's kart.

Don't think about it.

Final lap.

Chequered flag. Ollie swinging out to try to overtake me. I crossed the line ahead of him.

I'd won.

Weird, I felt let down — as if Craig had taken something away. I'd wanted to beat him fair and square.

Then I thought about the heats and the pre-final. I'd driven beyond my normal limits in all three of those races. He'd made me push myself further than I knew I could go.

By the time I rolled into the pits, put the kart across the scales and climbed out, the reality of the win had kicked in. I was leading the Challenge — and I deserved to be leading.

Felix leapt at me, knocking his head against my rib protectors. 'Archie! You won! *Awesome!*'

Dad and Grandad had identical pleased expressions on their faces.

'You earned that win, Archie,' Dad said.

I grinned back at him. 'How did Craig go?'

'Achieved his aim, I think,' Dad said dryly. 'He

knocked Silver off the track. Probably lost him a few places too. He came in sixteenth.'

'She might put in a protest,' I said. Craig would, if she'd done it to him. It was hard to know what Silver would do.

Gran had the afternoon tea ready and waiting when we got back to the tent. I was scoffing my second slice of bacon and egg pie when Dad said, 'Pick up your cup, Archie. We need to drink a toast to Felix.'

'Huh? Why?'

Felix was puzzled too. 'Archie won the race. We should say congratulations to Archie.'

Grandad said, 'We'll do that later. But cheers to you first, Felix. You asked if Craig was cheating. Got us thinking.'

'You talked to the stewards?' The surprises were sure coming thick and fast today.

'Just dropped a word in the right place,' Dad said. 'I suggested they have a look at his previous lap times and compare them with today's. With yours too. You drove bloody well, by the way. Best you've ever done.'

We lifted our cups. 'Cheers, Felix.'

'Thanks, bro,' I said.

Ever seen a grin split a kid's face in half?

Jack erupted into the tent. 'Old man Bateman's sacked Gus! He's gone storming off, so the old man has to get the caravan home himself.'

'Tell him you'll drive the Audi back for him,' I said.

It took Jack a couple of seconds to remember he didn't have the right sort of licence to drive on the road.

Nobody was surprised that, for the second time, Craig and his father hadn't waited around for prize-giving. I gave the obligatory speech, thanking my sponsors for the tyres, Gran for the food, Dad, Grandad and my bro Felix for the technical expertise. He won a spot prize. It was a helmet. He was over the moon and up among the planets. Dad muttered, 'The fat will be in the fire now.'

Yes. Erica wouldn't be quite as ecstatic as her son was. Dad cunningly let him ring her to tell her. Then he took the phone back and had a few minutes' conversation where he took himself off to where we couldn't hear. The rest of us got on with packing up.

We said our goodbyes to Gran and Grandad, then hit the road. As we were coming down the Bombay hills, Dad asked, 'You sore?'

'Just the usual. No worries.' But I did hurt more than usual. Poor old body, it always took a battering during a race day. No suspension. G-forces. Bruising. I didn't regret a single ache and I would do it all over again next month in Rotorua.

CHAPTER THIRTY

IT WASN'T A helluva lot of fun getting up for school in the morning. When I made it to the kitchen, there was Felix all bright and bubbling and wearing his helmet. Erica was wearing a strained expression. Dad was generating calm. All fairly normal.

At school, I caught up with my friends at interval to find Nina and Ginnie doing one of those useless *does so/ does not* arguments.

Nina: 'Hexes do so work.'

Ginnie: 'They so do not.'

'Do so.'

'Do not.'

Then Nina turned to me. 'It did work, didn't it Archie? You won. Therefore my hex is powerful.'

'Hate to break it to you, Nina. But I won because Craig got caught bending the rules.'

They gaped at me. 'Cheating?' Colin asked. 'Disqualified?'

'Yeah. Both.'

Nina took a breath, but James silenced her. A hand across your mouth will do that. 'Shut it, Nina. Tell all, Archie.'

I gave them the whole story. Ginnie said, 'Too full of himself. I bet anything you like it never entered his head that he'd get caught.'

She was probably right. I wondered how many other times Gus had 'helped' a driver win.

I talked about it that night with Kyla. But not for long. I'd had enough of Craig.

A week later, though, he was back on Facebook, doing the grand apology. This one was longer than the one he'd offered Silver. *To all my fellow karters I want to say how sorry I am that I let my mechanic talk me into an illegal set-up. I can see now that it was stupid and I should have sent him down the road right then and there. Please accept this apology and my promise that I'll never do anything that dumb ever again.*

Sel skyped me. 'What d'you think about the Great Grovel?'

'It's typical — not his fault, apparently. Gus gets all the blame. He should have just said *Sorry I got caught.* I'd believe that.'

Sel laughed. 'Exactly what I think. Can't wait to see if he shows up at Rotorua.'

'You'll be there?' It was a long and expensive journey from Dunedin, especially when he didn't have a realistic chance of winning.

'Wouldn't miss it for anything. We're having a blast, me and the old man.'

Me and my old man were having a blast too. Neither of us said so, but we could both feel the possibility of the trip to Portugal hovering just around the corner. For those four weeks between Auckland and Rotorua, Dad neglected Erica to work on the kart with me. Felix deserted his mother as well. He only stopped wearing his helmet to work in when he discovered it got in the way too much.

We did everything we could to get the optimum

set-up for the kart. Took it to get it balanced, then on Wednesday of the week coming up to Rotorua we went out to the track to make sure everything was perfect. It wasn't. There was something wrong with the engine. We took it off and gave the back-up one a run. It was okay, but it was a fraction slower than the good one. The kart itself, though, was perfect.

'Bloody engine,' Dad said. 'Don't worry, Archie. I promise we'll get it right before tomorrow.' The day we were driving up to Rotorua.

Dad and I worked on it after dinner, but Erica sent Felix to bed. 'Now. Or you don't go to Rotorua.'

No more argument from the kid, but a grumpy face can say a lot.

Dad sent me to bed at ten o'clock. 'Tired drivers make mistakes. Off you go, Archie. And don't worry. I've got a few ideas still to try.'

But I woke up early next morning to the noise of the engine. It still sounded rough. I leapt out of bed, remembered to throw on some clothes and raced to the garage.

'Dad? It's no better?'

He grunted. 'It will be. I've got Grandad on the case. You get off to school. Stop worrying.'

'Are you okay?' His face was a sickly shade of pale.

'I'm fine. Nothing to worry about. Get off to school.'

Nothing to worry about? He sure didn't look too flash. But I didn't want to get my head bitten off, so I didn't ask for details.

When Erica came out to the kitchen, I said, 'Dad doesn't look too good.'

She pulled a face. 'Getting to bed at two, then getting up again at five can leave you looking like a rag.'

She was right pissed off, so I got on with eating my breakfast and took myself off to school.

But my head wasn't tuned to class work. What if Dad really was sick? What if he couldn't fix the engine? At interval, I rang him. He sounded cheerful. 'Listen to this, Archie.' The roar of the engine battered my eardrum. I held the phone away so that I could listen properly. Yes! It was smooth, not a cough or a wobble.

'Sounds good, Dad,' I yelled.

He must have heard, because he shut the engine down. 'It was all just a matter of making small adjustments. Things must have got out of kilter when we took it down for balancing.'

'Phew! Brilliant. Thanks, Dad. I'll get home quick as I can. Felix can help me get everything packed.' Could be good to let Dad spend some time with Erica, since he'd been neglecting her for the past few weeks.

But he said, 'I'm taking the day off. I'll do it.' He hung up before I could suggest he should have a sleep. Probably would have snapped my head off — he doesn't like being told what to do, and he hates sleeping during the day.

Colin spent the rest of interval making engine noises. A Ferrari, he reckoned. 'A sick one,' Silas said.

The girls got fed up and disappeared. Yeah, a bad Ferrari noise can be slightly irritating. By contrast, the bell was music. We had maths. I practised focusing, and some of it stuck to the brain.

I rang Dad again at lunchtime. He didn't answer. I rang the landline till the answerphone picked up. He could be having lunch somewhere with Erica — except that she'd be at work and he hadn't arranged to meet her, as far as I knew. He'd looked bloody awful this morning too. What if . . . I jogged towards the bike sheds.

'Archie! Where the feck d'you think you're going?' Colin's bell-like voice.

'Home. I'll be back in time for class.'

I heard Ginnie say, 'Let him go. His head's not here anyway.'

I rode fast but carefully. An accident now wouldn't be a great idea. Dad would be fine. He'd laugh at me for worrying, then he'd yell at me and tell me to get back to school. I hoped.

The van was parked in the driveway, so he must be at home. I opened the front door. 'Dad?' No answer — and there wasn't any noise coming from the garage. I went in anyway. 'Dad?' He wasn't there. The kart was on the stand and the trailer door was open. I looked around.

'Oh my god! Dad!'

He was lying on the floor with his head in a pool of blood, one leg skewed under him. I dropped to my knees beside him.

'Dad?' I put my ear against his chest. Nearly howled with relief. His heart was beating. He wasn't dead. *Erica. Phone Erica. No. Ambulance first.* I dialled 111. Gave them the details. 'Hold a clean cloth against the wound,' they told me. 'But don't move him.'

The wound had to be on the side he was lying on, but if it was dangerous to move him . . . I ripped off my shirt, folded it into a skinny pad and eased it under his head. Then I called Erica.

'It's Dad. He's breathing, but he's passed out on the floor. He's cut his head.'

'Call the ambulance. I'll be there as quick as I can.'

She hung up before I could tell her I'd already rung

for the ambos, but the truth was, I'd be bloody glad to see her.

The ambos arrived after what seemed like ages. They put a neck brace on Dad before they moved him. 'Good work with the shirt,' the older ambo said.

'He's done some damage to his ankle,' the other one said as she wrapped a splint around it.

Erica tore in. 'What's happened? Bill?'

The ambos stared at her. 'Dr E! What are you doing here?'

I answered for her, because she was busy giving Dad the once-over. They didn't seem to mind. 'She's a good doc,' the woman said. 'One of the best. If you've got to have an accident, have it while she's on duty.'

Erica straightened up and turned to me. 'He's coming round. Thank heavens you came home, Archie. And I'm sorry I snapped at you this morning. You were right — he wasn't well. I should have asked him what was wrong.' She stepped back to let the ambos stretcher him away.

'He wouldn't have told you. He never admits he's sick. Erica — is he really going to be all right?' Now that the cavalry had everything in hand, I'd got the shakes.

She gave me a brief hug. 'Yes. We'll need to find out what made him pass out, though. There's a number of things it could be. Don't worry, I'll get to the reason.'

Bloody hell, it was just like tuning an engine. And that's when it struck me — he wouldn't be able to drive the van up to Rotorua this afternoon.

CHAPTER THIRTY-ONE

ERICA AND I followed the ambulance to the hospital. Worry about Dad chased around in my head, competing for space with the gut-wrenching disappointment about not getting to Rotorua. The only other person who could drive me was Grandad — but he was in Tauranga and I needed to leave today. Not possible.

I sighed.

Erica patted my hand. 'He'll be all right, Archie. He'll have come round properly by now. Won't be impressed to find himself in the Emergency Room either.'

An arriving text saved me from having to answer. It was Colin. *Where the hell r u? Taylor wil hav yr ars.*

I texted back: *Following dad to hosp in ambulance. Wil be ok. Gave me heluva scare.*

Mate! I tel Mr T.

Thanx

Erica parked the car, then leapt out and disappeared, leaving me to make my own way. When I found the right place, I had to laugh. Dad was lying propped up on pillows on a skinny little bed, glaring at a bunch of medics around him. A couple of them were arguing with Erica. 'You do not treat members of your own family,

Erica. Step back and let us get the job done.'

Hell, but she looked just like Felix at his most stubborn. Then something must have clicked into place and she stepped back. She saw me and came over. 'He's awake and insisting he's fine. Not a thing wrong with him. A huge panic about nothing.' She snapped her mouth shut.

'What made him pass out? Will they find out?'

'If they don't, I promise you I will. He's going to have to take it quietly for a few days.' She must've seen my face drop, because she said, 'Oh! Archie, I'm so sorry. But it'd be madness for him to drive anywhere at the moment. There's his foot too. It looks like there's bad bruising at the very least.'

'I'm just glad he's not dead.' I couldn't say any more — I'd bawl if I tried.

'Me too. Grab us both a cup of something, will you? And a bite to eat.' She handed me a twenty. 'There's a coffee bar in the entry foyer. Could you get me a long black and an egg sandwich? They do good ones.'

Old Erica, she knew her stuff. Giving me something to do — that was gold.

I had to wait while they made her coffee, so by the time I got back to where I'd left Dad, there was no sign of him. Erica was easy to find, though. She was frowning over a chart and talking to a woman lying on a bed.

I hung back, not wanting to get in the way, but she saw me, said something to the woman and came over. 'Thanks, Archie. Your dad's going to be fine. He's got an inner ear infection that upset his balance. He said he tripped on something — remembers falling and the next thing he knew he was in the ambulance.'

I let out a long breath. 'That doesn't sound too serious?'

She gave me a reassuring smile. 'He'll be good as new in a few days. Except for his ankle. He's waiting in X-ray now, but it looks to me like he's broken something.' She reached out to touch my arm. 'I'm so sorry about the race.'

I shrugged. Didn't want to talk about it. 'Can I wait with Dad?'

'He said for you to go back to school. It'll be better than waiting round here.'

My reading of it was that Dad didn't want any of us sitting by his bed, worrying and fussing. But I shook my head. 'Can't face school. I'll go home. I'll collect Felix too.'

She gasped. 'Oh lordy! Can you believe it! I forgot Bill was going to pick him up.' She looked like she was going to cry.

'A lot's been happening,' I said. 'Okay if I use the rest of that twenty for the bus fare?'

WE'D LEFT THE house unlocked, but everything seemed okay. The pool of blood in the garage had turned sticky, but I cleaned it up as best I could, then for something to do I finished getting the trailer and my gear ready. A part of me still hoped for a miracle. Dad might be well enough to drive by tomorrow, and we'd get there if we left early enough. His ankle might look a lot worse than it was.

But saying it out loud when I broke the news to Felix made me accept that it wasn't going to happen. He bawled, just like I'd been wanting to do all afternoon.

We were sitting at the kitchen table, trying to get up the energy to start cooking, when Dad and Erica arrived home. Felix stared at the pad of bandage on Dad's head, and we both stared at the boot affair on his ankle. Erica held one of his arms, and he had a crutch on the other.

'Sorry, son. Bloody stupid thing to do.' He gave a sigh of relief as Erica helped him lie down on the sofa in the lounge. 'Bloody head. Dizzy as hell when I move.'

He missed the grin I'd persuaded to wobble on to my face because he'd shut his eyes. 'Just don't go playing dead on me again.'

Felix huddled into his mother, tears still dripping. 'Don't die, Bill. Please don't die.'

'I've still got a few miles left on the clock, Felix. I'll be around for a while yet.'

Erica rubbed at her face and cleared her throat. 'I have to think. Three nights. What do I need? And you boys need to get a move on too. Felix, go and pack your bag. Archie — can you get things ready for us to leave as soon as possible.'

I screwed up my eyes. 'What? Are you coming too? But Dad can't . . .'

She had that determined look on her face. 'No, he can't. But I can.'

For the second time that day, my legs gave way and I plonked down into a handy chair. Hope was having a ding-dong battle with disbelief. 'You mean you—'

This time she smiled. 'It's all arranged. I'll drive. I've got leave from work. Felix's carer is going to stay with Bill.'

Felix, just about chopping her in half with his hug, shouted, 'Mum! You're *awesome*!' and sped off to his room.

I hadn't succeeded in getting myself upright, so I just

sat there, probably looking as if I'd been knocked on the head as well. Then, bugger me if I didn't start to cry.

She just handed me the tissues and said, 'I agree. It's been quite a day.'

I got the tear ducts shut down. 'Thanks, Erica.' I shook my head. That sounded so weak, so inadequate, so I tried again. 'Thanks.' Still pathetic, but she got the picture.

'I'd like to leave in half an hour if you can get things organised by then.'

That got the legs working. Dad, his eyes shut again, said, 'Ring Grandad. He'll have to be your guardian for the event. He won't mind.'

That was an understatement. 'You tell that son of mine not to worry. We'll be there with bells on,' Grandad said.

Twenty-five minutes later, just as we were about to head off, there was a thumping great bashing on the front door.

'That's got to be Colin.' I went to open it before he knocked a hole in it. Yep. Colin, along with Silas, James, Nina and Ginnie, all of them looking worried.

'How's your dad?'

'Is he driving you?'

'What happened?'

I clapped my hands over my ears. 'Whoa! One at a time. Or how about you all shut up and let me talk?' But I was chuffed that they'd come. I gave them the short version of events and finished with, 'You just caught me. Erica's driving and we're leaving now.'

The girls gave me good-luck hugs. The guys did the high fives and issued orders to text the results. 'You'll suffer if you don't,' Colin said.

'I'll do my best to remember. Give my love to school tomorrow.'

'We'll tell old Taylor you sent him a kiss,' Colin said. The bugger — he just might do that.

They disappeared, laughing, just as Diane, Felix's carer, arrived. I led her through to the lounge, where Dad was sprawled on the sofa, his eyes shut. He didn't look great. God, I hoped Erica was right and that he'd be better in a day or two.

We said our goodbyes. Dad just grunted, then said, 'Do your best, Archie. Good luck, mate.'

A few minutes later we were on our way. Erica drove slowly, her hands scrunched tight from nervousness on the wheel. She'd wear herself out if she couldn't relax a bit. I only just managed to stop myself from offering to do some of the driving. Ironical that the law wouldn't let me. I knew she'd say no, and I for sure didn't want to upset her.

'We'll stop at Waiouru for dinner and stay in Taupo tonight,' she said. 'I'm afraid it'll mean an early start in the morning.'

'No problem,' I said. 'That's absolutely no problem.'

Felix said, 'Mum, you're driving the trailer. I didn't know you could do that.'

'Neither did I,' she muttered. 'You realise I've never even towed a tiny trailer before?'

'You're doing fine,' I said. 'And I don't care if you want to crawl along at 30 ks. Just so long as we get there.'

She didn't go that slowly and her confidence improved once we hit the open road. Felix did his usual commentary throughout — names and kart numbers flying out of his mouth. Eventually, Erica asked, 'Is he always like this?'

'No,' I said. 'Sometimes he goes to sleep.'

She took a peek at him via the rear-view mirror. 'Felix, honey, you're going to have to explain who all these people are. Why might Craig not turn up? Why does Archie have to watch out for Silver? Why do you think Jack will take a picnic on the grass? Why would he do that?'

He didn't need any more encouragement. She listened, every so often shaking her head, but she looked happy enough and her hands relaxed on the steering wheel.

We stopped for burgers at Waiouru. Erica flexed her shoulders and drank two cups of coffee. We got back on the road. Felix stayed awake until just before we pulled up at the motel in Taupo, where Erica and I carried him inside and dumped him on a bed.

'He's getting heavy,' she said, tucking him in. 'He's come out of his shell so much since we moved in. A lot of that's thanks to you, Archie.'

'Looks like we're even then.' But before things could get too mushy I said, 'You must be tired. How about I make us a cuppa?'

I was going to race. I was still in the Challenge. Erica — she was going to make it happen. It was hard to get my head around.

CHAPTER
THIRTY-TWO

WE WERE ON the road by seven next morning, arriving at the track just after it opened. The grandparents were waiting for us.

'You're a real trooper,' said Gran, giving Erica a hug. 'We're so grateful.'

Erica said, 'You've got a good family, Janet. The best.'

Felix and I got busy helping Grandad with the tent. Gran moved out of the way, took Erica's arm and said, 'We'll leave you to get on with it.'

Erica looked worried, but Gran was firm. 'We'd only get in the way and clutter up the tent.'

No more argument from Erica.

Sel ambled up as I was getting into my overalls. 'Mr Big is here, all bright and shining. Probably thinks the grand apology fixed everything.'

I'd been too busy to think much about Craig.

'You watch out for him, Archie,' Felix said. 'I bet he tries cheating again.'

'Not much I can do about it if he does. But he'd be mad to try anything now. The stewards will be watching him.'

'His father must have found him a mechanic,'

Grandad said. 'I wonder if we'll get to meet him before he gets fired.'

Lucky for Craig, he behaved himself for the whole day. He pretty much kept to himself, too, though we did find out who his mechanic was — Dave Higgins, who owned a kart business in Christchurch. He told Jack's dad that Mr Bateman had made it worth his while but it was just for this one event. According to Jack, he'd said, 'Three days of that stuck-up little twerp are going to be all I can stomach.'

But we had more important things to think about. The track, for starters. It was a very technical track — the longest in the country. It was the fastest too and not one for the faint hearted. You had to keep your foot on the throttle, and winning often came down to a question of who had the most guts. We practised hard out all day, and nobody got in anybody else's way — not even Silver Adams. Could be she'd got tired of whatever game it was she'd been playing.

Grandad kept the kart perfectly tuned, Felix bounced around handing him tools and running errands. The two of them were having a ball.

When we were packing up for the night, Grandad said, 'Well?'

'Not too bad, I think. I've got the track pretty much in my head. I reckon I can post a good time in qualifying.' I refused to give head room to the knowledge that Craig raced regularly on this track.

Grandad drove us to the motel. It had its own private hot pool in the garden. Felix beat me into it, but not by much. I sat with water up to my neck, soaking out the soreness in my body. Heaven couldn't get better than this.

Felix wanted to eat his dinner in the pool. Not a happening thing apparently, so we both hauled ourselves out. Worth it, too. Some sort of casserole — more heaven. Then I went to bed. Soaking in a hot pool can make you tired. So can a full day of racing.

FELIX WAS THE first one awake in the morning. I know this because he was shouting before I'd even got my eyes open. 'It's raining. Archie, it's bloody raining!'

'Felix!' Erica called from her bedroom.

Oops. Guess who forgot his mother was on this trip?

Over breakfast, Grandad scowled at the weather, then did his best to reassure Felix, who wouldn't shut up about it. 'We'll handle it, Felix. Archie's first heat's not till this afternoon.'

Yes, we feckin' would handle it. I fired off a text to Dad. *On wets. Sure rains here.*

The sky was still tipping it down when we pulled out of the motel, and was even worse when we got to the track. We got to work swapping the tyres to wets and took the kart down to the grid, rain dribbling down our necks. Got to hand it to Felix — he didn't moan about it.

That bloody rain didn't let up. Even allowing for the wet track, I wasn't as quick as I should have been. 'It's probably the tyre pressures,' Grandad said. 'We'll put a bit more in the back. See if that makes a difference.'

It helped but it still wasn't right. We spent the morning tweaking it. Got it perfect for the first of the qualifiers.

I positioned myself in the middle of the field, aiming to let those in front of me get well ahead. I didn't want to drive with spray kicking up in my face. I made sure Silver was behind me, though. She'd been very low key all day so far — not her normal style at all. If she broke out, I didn't want to be anywhere near her. I kept away from Craig, too, but that was because I didn't want to have to talk to him.

It took a couple of wet, spray-filled laps before I got into the clear space I was after. *Time to drive.* I kept my foot on the throttle, then hard down on the brakes into the corners. All I had to do was make sure I was faster than any other bugger. Especially Craig. There was no way any of us would equal the course record today — 53.3 on a dry track. My best lap time was well short of that.

I cruised into the pits, hoping the rain would stop in time for the first heat.

I texted Dad at lunchtime, ending with: *Still raining. How you?*

Bored rigid. He must have been feeling better.

I handed the phone to Felix when the grid positions went up. 'Tell him I'm on pole, will you, Felix?'

Craig was on two, and three-tenths of a second slower.

My crew plodded through the puddles with the kart.

'Shit,' Felix said. 'It's raining harder.'

Grandad gave a bit of a grin but didn't growl at him for swearing.

Craig arrived just after I'd pushed my kart on to pole. We didn't talk, but it's easy not to chat when a waterfall is coming down on your head.

The starter, all dry and cosy under his big umbrella, let us go. Round we went until the lights gave the start signal. I accelerated, making sure I got the inside ahead of any fancy tricks Craig might try to pull. I had the lead and I kept it, lap after drenching lap. God knows what was going on behind me. The peripheral vision wasn't a lot of help in rain as solid as this was. I did see that three karts were off in the infield but gone by the time I came round again. Nothing major then.

Craig hassled me the entire race — just a bit more than was polite and gentlemanly. It made me more determined to keep him shut out from the lead. He popped up alongside me on every straight, steering in close, trying to make me change my line. But each corner, he had to fall back or take the inside line, which today was slippery as hell.

It was a bruiser of a race. Thump, bash all the way round. We came out of the high-speed ninety-degree last corner, accelerating down the straight to the finish line. He was right there beside me, rocking backwards and forwards to urge more speed. I crossed the line a nose in front.

Craig didn't speak to me when we got out. Grandad did, though, and loudly enough for Craig to hear. 'Got a bit rough out there, did it?'

'Nothing I couldn't handle.' I winked at Felix, who looked like he wanted to murder somebody, and no prizes for guessing who.

He shoved the phone at me. Dad's text read: *Good result. Get to bed early.*

'Good advice,' Grandad said.

Yeah. It was. I was tired, wet through, cold and amped. Me and my bro hit the hot pool as soon as we got back to the motel.

CHAPTER THIRTY-THREE

THE FIRST THING I heard in the morning was Felix hassling Erica. 'Mum, you're coming to the track today, aren't you? You have to see Archie race.'

Good luck with refusing that.

I got to the kitchen in time to see him do the forlorn puppy. She didn't look happy, but she said, 'Yes. I'll be there, darling.'

I said, 'Erica, you don't have to come. You've been brilliant. I'll never forget it.'

Felix wasn't impressed. 'You've got to come, Mum. You do. It's awesome. You'll love it.'

Gran said, 'We'll be there, Felix. We're just going to pick up something for lunch, but don't worry. We'll be there in time for Archie's heat.'

I looked at Erica.

'Don't worry about me, Archie,' she said. 'Bill's given me orders to keep him updated. I won't miss a thing.'

'Get cracking boys,' Grandad said. 'Time we were off.'

We went out into a grey day. It was hard to tell whether the rain was over or not.

We arrived ahead of Sel and Jack, but Craig, Josh,

Lewis and Ollie had got the jump on us. Not to worry — getting to the track first wasn't what it was all about.

Ollie and Lewis strolled into our tent. 'Had a chat with Craig yet?' Lewis asked.

'Haven't seen him. You?'

'He's hiding out in the van,' Ollie said. 'Not talking to anyone, I reckon.'

Fine by me. We went off to look over the track. We didn't talk much either. The track held all our attention. It would be fast today, a real test of driving ability.

As I was walking back to the tent, I saw Gran and Erica turning up, and just missed bumping right into Craig. 'Hey! Watch out!' he said, a friendly grin on his ugly mug.

I didn't feel entirely friendly. 'I'll watch out, Craig. You can be sure of that.'

He looked like he was going to grab my arm, but then he changed his mind. 'Come on, man. You're winning. What's your problem?'

I shrugged. He didn't get it. He probably never would. I went into our tent without saying anything else. Grandad chased me out again. 'Me and my offsider will do a hell of a lot better without you hanging over us.'

I removed myself, but stood in the entrance to take a long, hard look at the weather. Man, that sky was grey.

Sel and Jack ambled over. 'It's not going to rain,' Jack said. 'Betcha.'

'Happy to take your word for it,' I said. He could be right — he was local after all.

'Hey, have you heard who's finally decided to turn up?' Sel said. 'Silver Adams. Better late than never. Can't think why she keeps on coming. All she does is get in the way.'

'You know,' I said, 'I don't think I've heard her say a single word all year.'

Jack said, 'Damn lucky she's not fast enough to be up the front. She'd be a bloody nuisance.'

We laughed. The two of them were usually side by side on the grid, and both as loose as each other.

'Canteen?' Sel asked.

I shook my head. I wanted to be by myself for a bit.

They went in search of chocolate and orange juice, but I didn't move. I was watching Silver and her father come up from the parking area. It was the look on his face that made me stop. He looked like a man who'd gambled everything, and lost.

'Archie! What's wrong? You look like a stuffed dummy.' Gran prodded me — and hit a rib protector. 'Ouch! That'll teach me. Are you all right?'

'I'm fine.' I found a smile and stretched it out to take in Erica as well. 'Just thinking, that's all.'

'You're not worrying about Bill, are you?' she asked. 'He'll be up and about in a day or two. You'll see.'

I shook my head. 'No, it's not that. I just saw Silver's father. He looked . . . I dunno . . . desperate.'

'He is, the poor man,' Gran said. 'But you won't help by getting upset about it. Go and hang out with your mates.' She shooed me away, and I heard her filling Erica in about how Silver's mother had been killed.

I found a quiet spot trackside where I could tune my mind. Silver's dad — that look on his face. It had shaken me. The poor guy. It had to be all tied up with his wife's death and Silver's craziness.

Enough. Concentrate on the job in hand.

But my thoughts skipped right on to Craig. It wouldn't matter if he beat me today, because I just had to finish in the top three for the pre-final and final. If I could do that, the Challenge would be mine, and Dad and I would be on our way to Portugal. But I wanted to beat Craig. I wanted his guts on a plate.

And into my head popped one of Dad's rules: *Drive your own race. Don't worry about any other bugger.*

Yeah. Good idea. I got down to work, driving each corner in my mind, visualising the braking points, the entries and exits. By the time our heat was called, I was ready.

CHAPTER THIRTY-FOUR

IT FELT SO good to be pushing my kart on to pole for the second heat. Craig, beside me on two, wasn't chatty. Fine by me. Ollie and Lewis were behind us, with Josh back on five. Sel was on seven and stoked to be so far up the field. I didn't bother checking where Silver was, but she'd be somewhere near Jack, back around eighteen.

'Start your engines.' The starter counted us down and let us go. No problems in the rolling laps. I got a perfect start, accelerating the moment the lights went out, leaving Craig scrambling around behind me. With part of my mind, I was waiting for the bumps to start as he hunted me into the corners. There was nothing. I focused on my own race.

Be consistent. Stay on the track.

He was there right behind me, though, and popping up in my peripheral vision on the straights. Lap six, there was an almighty thump on the back of the kart — not enough to shove me off, but bad enough to send the kart shimmying sideways into the exit. And that's when Craig nipped past me.

Cheating dipstick loser. You won't get away with this.

Right then I heard Dad's voice again: *Drive your own race, Archie.*

Yes. It'd be the dumbest move ever to throw away my trip to Portugal just for the sake of revenge. So I drove my own race, hard out and back in the state where you don't make conscious decisions. You just drive.

Craig went wide a couple of laps later on the sweeper, leaving the door open for me to sneak through on the inside. He'd have to stay wide to let me through. That was the rule.

He broke the rule. He turned down across the nose of my kart and sent us both off the track. My kart slammed into the flag stand and came to a shuddering standstill, but he simply drove right back on to the track. I scrambled out, tugging at my kart to untangle it from the wooden stand.

One look was enough to tell me the kart was munted. The nose cone and Nassau panels — both smashed. Worse than that, it looked like the right stub axle was bent and the steering column hadn't come out of it too well either.

I started the engine. It sounded okay, not that it mattered. I stood looking at the mess, trying to accept that the day was over for me — and all hope of winning the Challenge gone. Sure, we could replace the nose cone and panel, but we didn't carry stub axles or steering columns.

Craig had taken me out deliberately. He couldn't win the Challenge, so he'd made sure I wouldn't either. I thought about putting in a protest. Useless. He'd just have to say his kart hit a patch of oil and he lost control, or some other unlikely story. Even if the protest got upheld, it wouldn't alter the fact that I was out. I burned with a cold, savage fury. I knew that soon it would change to biting disappointment. Give me fury any day. I swear if Craig had come near me right then, he'd have got himself every bit as mangled as my kart was.

The race finished. Lewis won, followed by Josh, then Ollie. Craig was fifth, not that I cared.

By the time the truck came to collect me and the bits of my kart, my anger had turned the corner into black disappointment. And my feet were kicking up a fuss where fecking Craig had run over them.

Grandad greeted me with, 'Can we fix it?'

I just shook my head.

He took a look anyway. 'Engine okay?'

I nodded. Not that it mattered.

A steward helped him lift the kart on to my trolley. Felix helped too, sobbing his heart out. *Go for it, Felix.*

Halfway back to base, Grandad said, 'We haven't got the parts, Archie.'

I got my voice working. 'Yeah. I know.'

Grandad swore all the rest of the way. The good thing was that it made Felix stop crying. I knew my mates were all there, watching us, but they had the good sense not to say anything — except for Jack, who said, 'Want us to knee-cap him for you, Archie?'

I just waved a hand at him. Nice thought.

We'd just about reached the tent when who should come running up but the last person I wanted to see right then. Actually, scratch that — Craig Bateman would be worse. But Silver Adams was up there on the *don't want to see* list.

She spoke. Actual words came out of her mouth. And they stopped me dead. 'Archie. Take my kart. Use what you need.'

I stared at her and I knew my mouth was open. 'What?' I managed to say. 'Why?'

'Just take it!' She turned to look behind her. Her father was pushing her kart towards us, his face all sad and despairing. *Man, I know how you feel.*

I shook my head. 'I can't drive your kart.'

She stamped her foot. 'Use the parts, you moron. Stop gawping. There isn't much time if you want to beat that heap of shit.'

Something in me snapped. Everything just piled in on top of me and I lost it. 'Why?' I didn't quite yell at her, but near enough. 'If it means so fecking much to you to beat Craig, then *you* go out there and do it.'

She reached out, snatched hold of my arm and started shaking it. 'You don't understand. Just do it. Take my kart. You can beat him. You can.'

I dragged my arm free. 'Why? This is all about your mother, isn't it? Your mind is seriously twisted, sister. Your mum's still going to be dead even if I do beat him.' Shit. I wanted to take that back. Too late now. And there she was looking at me, her eyes suddenly stark in a dead white face.

I took a breath to apologise just as she gasped out a few words. 'My mother . . . she's . . . it was my fault. I shouldn't . . .' Then she collapsed down on to the ground, sobbing out words I couldn't decipher.

My god, what had I done? I looked at Silver's father. But he gave the trolley a push in my direction. 'Take it, Archie. And thank you. From the bottom of my heart, thank you.'

That was enough for Grandad. 'Come on, Felix. We've got work to do.' The two of them pushed her kart into our tent.

Erica and Gran knelt beside Silver. Erica put her arm under Silver's shoulder and heaved her up. Gran looked at me. 'Hop it, Archie. We'll take over here.'

Well, okay, I guess. I didn't understand any of it — not why Silver had suddenly got talkative, or why she'd started howling like an engine in pain. Or why her dad was now looking like he'd won something precious.

Hop it, Gran had said. But my feet ached. Just something else to niggle when I drove, but they'd be bruised, that was all. Could Grandad really get my kart going in time? If he did, I'd be well back in the field, probably around twelve or fourteen. I let in a trickle of hope.

I was still standing there doing my stuffed dummy impersonation when three people showed up. The first one was Dave Higgins, Craig's current mechanic. He nodded to me but went straight into the tent. I stuck my head in, just a bit curious to hear why he'd come.

'Dick Bateman said you might like a hand.'

Grandad glanced up. 'He's paying you?'

'Only for today. I'm straight. There'll be no funny business.'

'Good. Thanks.'

Another trickle of hope joined the first one. There was a small stream there by now, but it gurgled to a halt as I caught sight of my next visitors. A steward, followed by the first-aid guy.

I got in first. 'I'm fine.'

'He ran over your feet,' the steward said. 'You know the score, Archie. Boots off, please.'

I had to go to the ambulance, where my feet got prodded and pushed in various directions. All of them hurt, but every time the first-aid guy asked, 'Does that hurt?' I said no it was fine.

'Liar, but it's your funeral and nothing seems broken.' He clapped me on the back. 'Good luck to you, Archie. You're a fine driver. You deserve to win.'

A comment like that can make a bloke come over all emotional. I muttered a thank you and got out of there, doing my best not to limp.

I walked slap bang into a posse of my mates. 'What's up?'

'We heard something about Silver.'

'Craig's old man is spitting mad at him.'

Jack shouldered his way to the front and held up his hands. 'Hold it, lads. Let the boy speak, for chrissakes.'

So I spoke, but none of them had any ideas about what made Silver Adams tick either. They all wished me luck, ending with some variation of 'Nail that fecker's nuts to the floor.'

They drifted off to their bases, their heads already occupied with the pre-final to come. I was too scared to go anywhere near our base. What if they couldn't reassemble my kart? Even if they could, how would it go on the track? I wouldn't be able to try it out. My thoughts chased round and round until Felix came running out, carrying a phone.

'It's Bill. He says what the bloody hell is happening and why hasn't anybody texted him.'

I took the phone. 'Calm down, Dad. There's been some drama here.' I filled him in on the details, then asked, 'How are you?'

'Having a heart attack here waiting for news. What the hell's Erica playing at? She promised to keep me up with the play.'

'She and Gran took Silver off somewhere. Don't yell at her, Dad. She's awesome.' I gave Felix a grin.

Dad muttered something, then he said, 'Do your race prep, Archie. Treat it like a normal pre-final. Focus.'

I said goodbye and gave the phone back to Felix. 'Thanks, mate.'

◉

AS USUAL, DAD was right on the money. I set about ditching all the drama from my thoughts and bringing my focus to the race ahead. But the knowledge lurked that maybe they couldn't get my kart fixed in time.

The pre-final announcement crackled out from the speakers. Already? No way would they have been able to reassemble my kart so soon.

I had to force myself to go back to the tent.

The first thing I heard was the engine, running sweetly. I hobbled faster. Three jubilant faces greeted me. 'You've fixed it? Really?'

Dave switched off the engine. 'It'll get you round the track, Archie. More than that we can't promise.'

I stood there, grinning like an idiot. 'Thanks, guys. I'll do my best. You're amazing. All of you.'

Felix shoved my helmet at me. 'Get moving, Archie. You have to grid up.'

Bossy little rat. He was having the time of his life.

Down at the grid, I pushed my kart on to thirteen, my mind already busy with how I'd drive the start.

The starter flagged us away and I used the two rolling laps to test the kart as much as I could. It wasn't perfect and would probably be worse at speed. The track was dry now too, and getting faster with each race.

We approached the start — and I had to laugh. Ahead of me, my mates were all over the track instead of neatly formed up in their positions and ready to race. Round we had to go again. Craig would be furious. They'd done it on purpose to give me an extra lap to test the kart. I made good use of it, throwing the kart into the corners to try to work out how to compensate for the slight drag at the back. The drivers around me kept out of my way.

By the time we came up to the start again, I was feeling more confident. And I had a plan — I'd drive it like I'd stolen it.

CHAPTER THIRTY-FIVE

THE LIGHTS WENT out, my foot went down on the gas. The karts ahead of me were slower, and I made up four places before the turn, snaking my way through the gaps, seeing them almost before they opened. I snuck past another kart on the hairpin, picking off the middle bunch one by one over the next couple of laps.

The leading pack of Josh, Ollie, Lewis and Craig were tightly bunched. I followed them round, waiting for my chance, compensating in every turn for the drag at the back. Craig was driving like a demon. He'd made up three places and now only had Lewis in front of him.

Drive your own race.

Ahead of me, Josh tried sneaking through to pass Ollie, went too far into the greasy part of the seal and spun off. I kept out of the way and ducked under on the inside, getting past Ollie. Had to fight to keep the kart steady as the inside wheels caught the edge of the slippery stuff. He played by the rules and let me through.

Only Lewis and Craig ahead of me now. I could wait this out. Sit tight and just make sure I came in third.

No. Beat that sniveller. Grind him into the dirt.

I missed my braking point on one of the infield

hairpins. I was very lucky that it didn't cost me a place.

Concentrate. Get into the zone.

I drove the last couple of laps alert for any chance to overtake, but there were none. Third. Not too bad.

Grandad met me with, 'What's it doing?'

'A bit of drag on the back. Apart from that, it's a fecking miracle.'

'Can we fix it, Grandad?' Felix asked, his eyes so big and worried they almost swallowed his face.

'We can fix it, mate.' Then to me he said, 'All you have to do is stay in third place, Archie. No heroics. Be consistent.'

'Yeah. I know.' And we both knew I'd go hard out and do everything, except cheat, to win that final. 'How's Silver?'

Grandad shrugged. 'Don't know. They haven't come back.'

Felix kicked a trolley tyre. 'It's not fair. Mum promised she'd watch. She *promised*.'

'A lot of things aren't fair, my lad,' Grandad said. 'Your mum's probably helping save that girl's sanity. Or her life. None of us would be here if your mum hadn't stepped up, so no more grizzles from you. Understood?'

Felix dropped his head. Possibly to hide tears.

'Chin up,' Grandad said. 'We've got work to do, you and me.'

That chirped Felix up.

Dave Higgins joined us as we reached our tent. 'Shouldn't you be helping Craig?' Grandad asked.

Dave smiled. 'His dad's not so happy with him. Told me to make sure everything's good here and then if there's any time left Craig can have my undivided attention.'

'Pity it's taken him fifteen years to thump sense into that boy,' Grandad said. 'Thanks, Dave. Archie — go and get yourself fuelled up in the canteen.'

I was pleased to go, even though it meant walking on my throbbing feet. But the usual body parts were all kicking up a fuss by now anyway, so what did a couple more matter? Quite a lot. They ached like stink.

Sel and Jack were already there, plates of food disappearing down their gobs. I got spag bol and joined them. Ollie, Josh and Lewis came in a couple of minutes later. We talked about the racing, and then about Silver, but none of us said too much. She was one large question mark, that girl. We didn't mention Craig either. Best not to go there.

Then, what do you know — he strolls in as if he was still king of the dung heap. He bought a drink, then sauntered over. 'The forecast says the rain will stay away. Good, eh?'

None of us responded.

I got up. 'See you on the track.' But I looked at my mates and not at Craig.

'I'm off too,' Sel said — and, with that, the others vanished as well, leaving Craig frowning at an empty table.

'He's lucky you didn't punch him, Archie,' Josh said when we were outside.

'And pollute my knuckles? Nah. He's not worth it.'

'He's unbelievable,' Lewis said. 'Turning up like that and expecting us all to ignore the fact that he's a cheating ball of slime.'

Jack squinted up at the sky. 'Hope he's right about the forecast, though.' The sky was dark. Looked to me like it would fall on us at any second.

They announced our final. Felix kept looking for his mother, but his mouth stayed shut. Silver must be in a bad way — Erica and Gran had been with her for ages. I hoped like hell she'd be okay. Poor cow.

I pushed my kart on to three, behind Craig. I spent a few moments trying to bend his chassis with the power of my mind, then I got to work doing my prep. This race would demand my total concentration for all twenty-seven laps. It was going to be long, and it was going to be hard. *Excellent.*

The starter counted us down and let us go. Craig set a steady pace for the rolling laps. Again, my mates made sure I got an extra lap to test my kart, and this time everything felt damn near perfect.

The lights went out. We were racing. I fell into the zone pretty much straight away — that state where the kart seems to know what to do all by itself. Where my mind computes all the variables of the race — track, other drivers, passing opportunities — all without conscious thought.

I passed Lewis on the top hairpin when he braked too soon. Craig was now only a kart length in front. I kept my concentration, stayed in the zone. I waited, patient, watchful and alert.

The chance came on lap 18. We came up to turn four. It was tight. I braked heavily. Craig did too, but again he went wide the way he'd done when he munted my kart. *Forget that.* I ducked through, watching him in my peripheral vision to make sure he gave me room.

I was through. He'd have to scramble to get out of that corner smoothly.

Stay in the zone.

Nine laps left, with Craig behind me, bumping my kart

every chance he got. I drove my own race, intent on staying on the track, on making sure I hit my braking points.

Six laps to go. I was leading. The steward counted the laps down. Five, four, three. I held the lead, driving hard out.

Second to last lap. The drizzle started. It was like driving on ice. I slowed just enough to ensure I stayed on the track. Had to change the line through every corner. No more bumps from Craig.

Final lap. Halfway round, the sky opened. Water bounced off the track, smacked into my visor, soaked me to the skin. I had a bad moment at corner seven — the sweeper that tightens up. Wrestled the kart and managed to stay off the grass. Nobody had passed me.

Hold it together. Three turns left.

Turn eight. Not tidy. Turn nine. I stayed on the track and was lucky to do so. I took the final turn — the high-speed right-hander — at half the usual speed. It'd be crazy to lose it now.

Down the finish straight, water all around me. I knew spray would be kicking up behind me. It might drown Craig. Nice thought.

And there was the chequered flag. I crossed the finish line, and all I knew was that nobody had beaten me. I took a quick look behind. Lewis was just crossing the line, with Ollie behind him. No Craig.

I'd won. I was going to Portugal to race. 'Yeee ha!' I took both hands off the wheel and punched the air. It was hard to believe.

I drove into the pits and on to the scales. 'Congratulations, Archie,' the steward said. 'I'm glad you won.'

Grandad and Felix came running in. 'You did it!'

Felix bellowed. 'Archie, you won! *Awesome!*'

Grandad squeezed my shoulder. 'Bloody good race, Archie. Fine driving. Damn fine driving.'

Lewis drove in next, followed by Ollie, with Josh not too far behind. 'What happened to Craig?' I asked. Not that I cared — just curious.

Grandad said, 'He went too fast into that final corner. Went straight off the end.'

'Dear dear,' Lewis said. He swiped water from his face with his gloves. Hard to tell which ended up dirtier — his face or the gloves. 'You drove a mean race, Archie. Sorry you beat me. Bloody glad you beat that cheating ball of slime.'

'Come on,' Grandad said. 'All you guys need to get dry. Get something warm into yourselves too.'

We left the karts to be checked, and sloshed back to our bases. Gran and Erica were waiting for us, hot Milo already steaming in mugs. Gran threw me a towel. It turned out every stitch I was wearing was drenched. I got changed in the trailer, pulling on my spare suit ready for prize-giving. *Prize-giving.* I'd won. It was starting to sink in.

I went back to the tent with a smile on my face.

'Mum watched the whole race,' Felix said. 'She thinks you're awesome.'

It could be time to teach that kid a different word, but not today because he was right. Erica was awesome. Today was awesome.

'You go so fast. I had no idea,' Erica said. 'And when the race started . . . I thought you'd be killed, Archie. I really did.'

'Nah, I know what I'm doing. But thanks for watching. You don't have to ever again.'

'I was surprised — it was really interesting. Nerve-wracking because we all wanted you to win, but I got drawn into the whole thing. I'm glad I saw it.'

I sipped my Milo and grinned at her. A phone went. Dad, of course.

'How are you feeling, Dad?'

'Stoked, son. Best medicine a bloke could have. Wish I could've been there. Or maybe not. Might have thumped that young jackass into the middle of next century.' With that, he hung up, which I figured meant he still wasn't feeling well and didn't want to talk about it.

'Is Silver okay? Can I see her? I want to tell her thanks for the kart.'

Erica shook her head. 'Her father's taken her home. She's a mess right now, but she's on her way to recovery.'

A wave of shame washed over me. 'I shouldn't have yelled at her. Can't believe I said that about her mother.'

'Archie, listen to me,' Erica said. 'You yelling that at her has probably saved her life. It shocked her so much it broke through the wall she'd built up. Her dad's been so worried about her that he never leaves her alone. Her aunt stays with them so she's never alone at night. The grandparents help out too.'

I gaped at her. 'They thought she'd kill herself?'

Gran nodded. 'Poor girl. It turns out she believed if she hadn't stopped to look in a shop window then her mother wouldn't have been standing in the path of that car.'

'Jeez, that's heavy. But I don't get how yelling at her . . .'

'She'd refused to talk about the accident, or about her mother,' Erica said. 'Her dad thought the racing might help her, and it did to some extent. But not enough, and he was facing that when you yelled at her.'

So that's why old man Adams had given me the kart like it was worth nothing to him. I wasn't totally sure how all that got mixed into Silver being desperate to make sure Craig didn't win — maybe she didn't know either.

I finished my drink. There was a lot to think about, but right now it was time to celebrate.

CHAPTER THIRTY-SIX

CRAIG CAME TO prize-giving. My guess was that his dad made him come. Mr Bateman looked stern. Craig looked at the floor. Mr B shook my hand. 'Congratulations, Archie. A well-deserved win.'

'Thanks. And thanks for letting Dave help with my kart.'

He just nodded and went back to sit beside Craig.

My turn came for the podium and the speech. I did the usual thanking of my sponsors, then went on, 'I owe today's win to the huge efforts of several people. I wouldn't have been able to get here if my fantastic step-mother Erica hadn't decided she really could drive a van and trailer all the way from Wellington. Grandad — you're an ace mechanic and bum-kicker.' I paused for the laughter to stop. Should I mention Craig's dastardly deeds, or not? Yeah, bugger it. He deserved to be showered with shit. 'I won't thank Craig for destroying my kart, but I do thank Dave for helping put it back together. And lastly I'm hugely grateful to Silver Adams for letting me use the parts off her kart. And, just in case anybody hadn't guessed, I'm totally stoked about winning the Challenge. Yay! I'm going to race in Portugal!'

I collected my trophy and we left as soon as we could after that. Erica wanted to get to Waiouru, stay there and leave early so we'd get home mid-morning.

Felix was ecstatic. 'You won, Archie. You beat that sniveller. You should have heard us cheer when you got past him. And then when he went off the track we cheered and clapped.'

We let him rave on. It was kind of peaceful, driving through the rain with him babbling away in the back seat. When sleep shut him up, Erica said, 'Are you tired, Archie?'

'Flat knackered. It's a demanding track, that one.'

'Will it be like that in Portugal?'

'No. There'll be way more karts on the track. More than seventy. I'd like to make it into the top twenty. I'll be rapt if I can do that.'

She drove without talking for a few ks and I was nearly nodding off myself when she said, 'I've never had to patch up a kart driver.'

I decided not to show her my feet, or to mention that they were aching up a storm.

She said, 'Rugby, soccer, tennis even. I've patched up injuries from all of them. Skiing and snowboarding — some really nasty breaks from those.' More silence for another couple of ks. 'He's so little.'

'I was six when I started racing,' I said. 'It's the best fun.'

'He might hate it,' she said.

I laughed. 'Are you going to let him have a go?'

More silent ks before she said, 'I might. I'll talk to Bill. It's a big step for me, Archie.'

'You're cool, Erica. You'll cope.' I spoke through a massive yawn.

'Go to sleep, Archie. But I'm not carrying you into the motel.'

'Walk, or sleep in the van?'

'You got it.'

⊙

DAD WAS STILL flat out on the sofa when we got home. 'I'm fine. Much better. Now sit yourselves down and talk me through the races.'

Erica gave him a kiss. 'Not me. I've got to start work in an hour.'

I needed to get to school too. So did Felix. But Erica just winked at me and left us to talk to Dad.

After lunch, I settled Felix on the bar of my bike and doubled him to school. He kept yelling, 'Go on, faster! Foot to the floor. Faster!'

That could well have answered Erica's doubts about whether or not he'd like racing.

I passed Mr Taylor on my way to maths. 'Congratulations, Archie. Well done.'

'Thanks, sir.'

So my friends had spread the word. Yep. They disrupted the lesson for the first few minutes by demanding to know all the gory details. Mrs Chin was a pretty relaxed teacher and she gave me the floor for about five minutes before she dragged us back to what we were meant to be doing.

I hadn't mentioned my bruised feet, but nothing gets past Ginnie. Straight after class, she asked, 'Why are you limping?'

'Because when another kart drives over your feet, it

buggers your own kart, plus there's collateral damage on your feet.'

'Show us,' Nina said.

I pulled the shoe and sock off my left foot, which had the prettiest bruises. They were properly impressed.

'You'll have to give the assembly talk,' Colin said, an evil grin on his face.

True. I'd forgotten about that. It was the downside of doing well at anything at our school — they hauled you up in front of assembly to explain what a red-hot dude you were. Or dude-ess.

I guessed it would happen on Wednesday, when we had senior assembly. I was right. I had to sit on the stage along with a Year 12 girl who'd won a writing prize and a Year 13 boy who'd beaten some top guy in a chess competition. They both did okay — even the chess guy. He was quite funny. That was a surprise.

I made my speech short. Thrilled to win, rah-de-rah sort of thing. But I finished with, 'I'm going to miss the exams, because I'll be racing in Portugal. I'll think of you all, though, slaving away here. Might even send you a postcard.'

I got booed rather than applauded.

BY THE WEEKEND Dad was up and around again, swearing at the boot he had to wear on his ankle. I made the mistake of asking if he thought he'd be fit enough to be my mechanic in Portugal. Nearly got my head snapped off. 'Three weeks away? Of course I will be. I'm fine. Stop your fussing.' It was so good to have him back to normal that I let him get away with a swift change of subject. 'We're having a celebration dinner tomorrow, Archie.'

'Your famous roast chicken with stuffing and gravy?'

'The works. But you and Felix will have to do the running around.'

What that turned out to mean was that he sat at the table and we did the work. Erica disappeared off somewhere but she promised to be back in time.

The kitchen was smelling wicked by the time she returned with sparkling apple juice for Felix and me, and champagne for her and Dad. I decided now wasn't the time to challenge the *no alcohol for minors* rule.

'Hey, Felix, we're damn good chefs,' I said, toasting him with a glass of too-sweet bubbles.

We were, too. The meal was perfection on a plate. Four plates to be exact. We all stuffed ourselves. 'I'm gunna bust if I have any more,' Felix said.

Dad shoved himself back from the table. 'Right, troops. Leave the dishes for now. Follow me.'

Felix looked at me. I shrugged — something was up, but I didn't have any idea what.

There was a suitcase on the lounge floor. A new one. With my name attached to it. 'For Portugal,' Dad said.

'Oh wow! Thanks, Dad. That's really cool.'

'Open it,' he said.

Inside was an envelope with an official type of form inside. 'A passport application! Good thinking, Dad.' There was something else in there too. Another envelope. With cash in it. I read the note that came with it. *This is to help you with your passport. Good luck for Portugal, darling. You've done so well. I'm proud of you. Love from Mum.*

I couldn't say anything for a moment or two. She was

proud of me. That was . . . good. Real good.

Felix got impatient. 'Open this one, Archie. It's from me and Mum.'

They'd given me a passport cover and a map of Portugal.

'Hey, are you sure it's not Christmas today? This is amazing. All of it. Thanks heaps.' We sat there smiling at each other.

Well, Felix didn't. He snatched a final parcel out of the suitcase. 'Open it, Archie.'

I shook my head and pointed at the name written on the paper. 'Read that, mate.'

'*Felix*. It's for me? Really?' But he was already ripping the paper off. 'It's a racing suit!' He held it in both hands, clasping it to his chest. 'Mum? It's a racing suit.' His eyes were doing that huge, swallow-his-face thing like he couldn't believe what he was seeing.

Erica smiled at him. 'You're going to need it for when you start racing.'

Well, that kid nearly knocked her flat, jumping at her to hug her. Happy families all round.

But Felix and I still got to do the dishes. He wasn't a lot of help because his head was somewhere far away in a land of fumes, noise and speed. I knew the feeling.

THAT NIGHT I talked to Kyla for ages. We had a lot to catch up on. I told her the whole gory story of Craig and how he'd tried to take me out. A lot of it — though not quite everything — had come out on various social media sites. But no one had said anything about Silver.

Kyla said, 'You haven't heard anything since you got home? About how she is now, I mean.'

'No. I messaged her to say thanks. No reply though. I'd just like to know she's okay.'

We tossed some ideas around about why it had mattered to her so much that Craig didn't win. 'Erica says he probably became the focus of her rage about her mother being killed.'

'Makes sense, I guess,' Kyla said. 'He was always a right shit to her.' Then she laughed. 'Hey, he did good in spite of himself.'

'That'd get right up his exhaust pipe. Hey, any chance of you coming up this way over the summer?'

Her face lit up. 'I'm working on it. Keep your fingers crossed. It's looking promising.'

We sat there grinning at each other, then she asked, 'When do you leave for Portugal?'

'Got the info yesterday. We fly out in three weeks. It's starting to feel real.'

I'd never been out of the country before. Actually, I'd only been on a plane once, and that was when I was quite young. I got little shivers of excitement every time I thought about it.

We'd do all the prep we could beforehand. Every competitor got supplied with a kart and all the gear, which meant all I could do to prepare was practise, read up everything I could about driving technique, study the map of the track we'd be racing on, and work on my fitness.

I'd thought the time would drag, but instead it took off at high speed, helped on its way by Dad sussing out a kart for Felix. We took him to the track to try it out. That kid was practically dizzy with excitement. It's a pity his mum had to work and couldn't see him.

Dad gave him some tips before he took off, but as soon as Felix left the grid, Dad said, 'He's too amped to take anything in. This should be interesting.'

His kart wasn't as powerful as mine but he would feel like he was jet-propelled. I still remembered the feeling of speed I'd got on my first few drives. I'd been certain I'd broken the sound barrier.

We watched Felix's progress — not too bad. He was driving at around half the speed the kart was capable of. 'He's doing okay in the corners,' I said.

'Should do. He's been a proper little sponge. He's absorbed all the stuff you've talked to him about.'

We waved him in after ten laps — it was like watching an approaching grin. 'I went fast! I reckon I could beat you, Archie! That was *awesome*!'

We didn't disillusion him.

He didn't talk much on the way home, but every now and again we'd hear *Awesome* from the back seat. He was asleep by the time we hit town.

THE WEEKEND BEFORE we left for Portugal, I had a sort of farewell event with my friends. We went rock climbing and then ate up large at a pizza place. At the end of the night, they wished me luck and threatened me with injury if I didn't keep them updated while I was away. Regarding injuries, Dad's leg was back in business and he was focused on getting us to Portugal. This apparently involved a few minutes telling his second-in-command at work to handle everything in his absence, and then reading up everything he could get his hands on about kart engines.

We were flying out on Wednesday morning. Erica drove us to the airport. Felix pulled my new suitcase and Dad walked with his arm around Erica. I didn't mind him doing that now. She was good value.

We did the goodbyes, then went through to the 'passengers only' part. We were on our way. I'd won this trip fair and square. I was going to race in Portugal.

PRESS RELEASE PUBLISHED ON *STUFF*

Wellington teen Archie Barrington has achieved a very creditable thirteenth placing in an international kart-racing competition in Portugal. His final placing was 13th out of 72. 'I'm very happy with that result,' Barrington says. 'The competition was fierce. It's been a fantastic experience. I was aiming to get into the top 20, so 13th is much better than I'd thought I could do. I'm stoked.'

ACKNOWLEDGEMENTS

Huge thanks to all the people who were so generous with their time and patience in answering my questions. Special thanks to: Donna and Ross Lee, Charmaine Jones, Andrew Donohue, Ryan Urban and Kylie, and Don McKenzie.

ABOUT THE AUTHOR

Fleur Beale is the author of many much-loved award-winning books — she has had more than 50 books published in New Zealand, the US and England. Fleur won the Storylines Gaelyn Gordon Award for a Much-Loved Book with *Slide the Corner* in 2007, the same award in 2009 for *I Am Not Esther* and the Esther Glen Award for *Juno of Taris* in the 2009 LIANZA Children's Book Awards. *Fierce September* was the Young Adult Fiction Category Award Winner at the 2011 New Zealand Post Children's Book Awards. Fleur also won the Margaret Mahy Medal in 2012.

OTHER BOOKS BY FLEUR BEALE

I Am Not Esther
A Respectable Girl
The Transformation of Minna Hargreaves
The End of the Alphabet
Juno of Taris
Fierce September
Heart of Danger
Dirt Bomb
The Boy in the Olive Grove

For more information about our titles
please visit www.randomhouse.co.nz